Pope Leo XIII, Woodstock College

The Latin Poems of Leo XIII

done into English verse by the Jesuits of Woodstock College. With a life of the

pontiff by Charles Piccirillo

Pope Leo XIII, Woodstock College

The Latin Poems of Leo XIII
done into English verse by the Jesuits of Woodstock College. With a life of the pontiff by Charles Piccirillo

ISBN/EAN: 9783337406714

Printed in Europe, USA, Canada, Australia, Japan

Cover: Foto ©Andreas Hilbeck / pixelio.de

More available books at **www.hansebooks.com**

LEONIS XIII

CARMINA

THE LATIN POEMS

OF

LEO XIII

DONE INTO ENGLISH VERSE

By the Jesuits of Woodstock College

PUBLISHED WITH THE APPROBATION OF
HIS HOLINESS

WITH A
LIFE OF THE PONTIFF
By Fr. Charles Piccirillo, S. J.

———

PEOPLE'S PUBLISHING CO., TORONTO.

1887.

LEONI · XIII

PONTIFICI · MAXIMO

STVDIORVM · OPTIMORVM

ALVMNIS · SACRORVM · INSTITVENDIS

VINDICI · ALTORI · PROVIDENTISSIMO

QVOS · IPSE · VERSVS · EXARAVIT

CANDIDAM · LATINITATIS · ELEGANTIAM

EXIMIE · REDOLENTES

EOS · IVNIORES · SODALES · E · SOC · IESV

QVI · IN · AEDIBVS · COLLEGII · WOODSTOCHIANI

PIETATI · STVDIIS · QVE · ADOLESCVNT

ANGLICE · A · SE · REDDITOS

FIDEI · ET · AMORIS · NON · EXIGVI

TENVE · PIGNVS

PARENTI · OPTIMO · INDVLGENTISSIMO

DEMISSO · ANIMO

OFFERVNT

P. CAROLUS PICCIRILLO, S. J.
STUD. MODER.

TO

OUR SOVEREIGN PONTIFF

LEO XIII,

WHO HAS WITH SUCH WISDOM AND FORESIGHT

ELEVATED THE EDUCATION AND TRAINING

OF THE YOUTH OF THE SANCTUARY,

THIS ENGLISH VERSION

OF HIS POEMS,

WHICH ARE REPLETE WITH THE SIMPLICITY AND GRACE

OF OLD LATINITY,

IS DEDICATED,

AS A MODEST TOKEN

OF THEIR GREAT LOVE AND FAITHFULNESS,

BY THE YOUNGER MEMBERS

OF THE SOCIETY OF JESUS,

WHO FROM EVERY PART

OF THESE UNITED STATES OF NORTH AMERICA

ARE COME TOGETHER FOR THEIR STUDIES

AT WOODSTOCK COLLEGE.

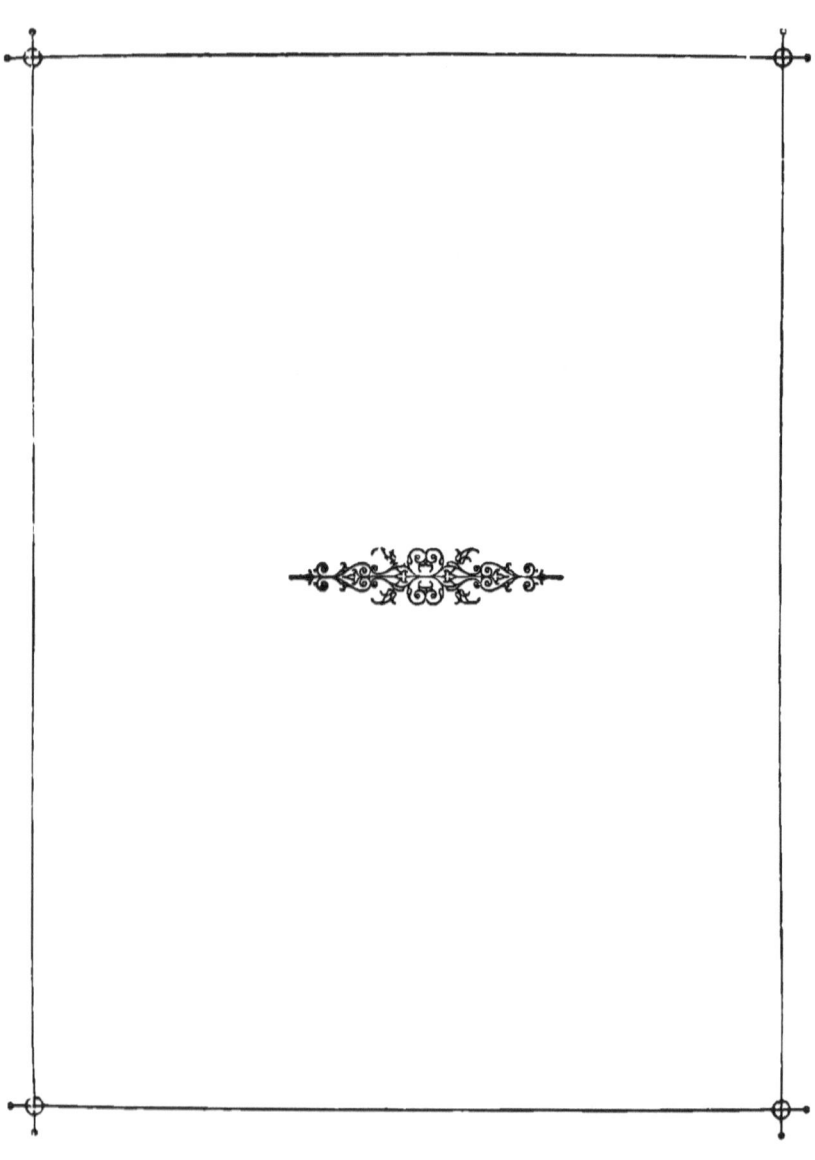

SKETCH

OF THE

LIFE

OF

LEO XIII.

Sketch

LIFE OF LEO XIII.

FROM Damasus to Leo XIII there have been Popes who wrote
poetry. For some of them it was merely an intellectual pastime;
for others it was a necessity. They sang, because their hearts
were full of song, because their natures were passionately fond of
truth and beauty and religion. But there is nothing professional
in such poetry. Men who are poets by profession write themselves, their own opinions, minds and hearts. We know them
from their books, and we can portray them very accurately from
the lines they have left us. But this is scarcely true of those who
write occasional verses; it is never true when they are men of
lofty position like the Popes. We should know nothing of Damasus, or of Sylvester, or of Urban, if we had only their verses to
judge them by. We should find, perhaps, here and there, through
their writings, many pretty thoughts; everywhere pious themes in
neat and elegant Latin; but their genius and sanctity would
nowhere appear. Our opinion of them would be that they were
good men who were masters of Latin diction.

So it is with the Latin poems of Leo XIII, which, side by side with an English version, we now offer to the public. They are so very few and with so little of distinctive character marked upon them, that the reader would never make out who their author was but for his name upon the title page. Such verses would tell that the author was an excellent Latinist, a man of gentle mind and religious feeling, with all Christian traits of character. All this Leo XIII is, and the Catholic prizes him for his scholarship and kindly heart and holiness. But there is more than learning and goodness in the character of Leo XIII. His Tiara has many jewels. Among the great men of the age his figure is prominent; and the world has come to think him the mightiest of crowned rulers. We have seen him lately arbitrating between Great Powers and respected as his predecessors were in the olden time. His person is clothed with all the majesty and some of the power that once made the Popes the marvel of the world.

We trust, therefore, that his poems will become more readily appreciated, if prefaced with a few pages of his life. We will give only the salient outlines, but they will be enough for our purpose. When the reader has been introduced to the author himself, he will take more interest in reading what otherwise might be considered merely elegant Latin verses. He will be prepared to understand the allusions and will be able to trace an affinity between these verses and the great unwritten poem—the life of Leo XIII.

The town of Carpineto, situated in Central Italy near Signia on the Lepine mountains, of no historical importance, though the Volscians built its walls centuries ago, has become famous as the birth-place of Pope Leo XIII, who was born there March 2nd,

1810. His parents wore Count Louis Pecci and Anna Prosperi, both of patrician blood, and of families that had given to the service of Church and State many able sons. It is true that nobility of birth is not a merit, but it is also true, that one of ancient lineage has the advantage over his fellows of humbler lot. His life-course is disclosed to him from the start, and he has the tradition of heroic deeds done by men of his blood to inspire him and urge him on to gain the heights, whether of sanctity or secular pride, which they aspired to and won.

Leo XIII was the youngest of four sons, one of whom, Joseph Pecci, is a member of the Sacred College of Cardinals, and his great learning, for he is a distinguished metaphysician and scientist, is sufficient warrant for his holding that high position. His Holiness was baptized Joachim, Vincent, Raphael, Aloysius, but his mother, through devotion to St. Vincent Ferrer, called him Vincent, and as such he was known to all, until his studies were finished, when he assumed his first name, Joachim. Madame Pecci was a very accomplished lady; she knew how to train her child, and the ambitious mother, even in those early days, planned a great future for her youngest boy. And who will say that she had no part in making the brilliant future that was really in store for him? She had him under her care only eight years; and yet in that short time her good work was done so thoroughly that, when he went forth alone, his young feet never strayed from the path she had marked out for them.

Vincent Pecci was only eight years of age, when he left his father's house and mother's arms to go to the Jesuit College at Viterbo and begin his course in Italian, Latin and Greek. He was a delicate boy, with that fine face, and those bright eyes which even seventy years have not dimmed, and which we yet admire in the portraits of Leo XIII. His manly character claimed the respect of all, while his bright mind made his companions look upon him as a prodigy. At thirteen he was studying his humanities under the able Jesuit, Father Leonard Giribaldi, and an old class-mate of Vincent, thus describes those early years, in a letter written to a friend, shortly after Leo's election to the Pontificate: " I assure you that when he was at Viterbo his clever mind and straightforward conduct made him a great favorite. We were together in the class of humanities, and though we fought each other for the honors, we were always good friends. He seemed the picture of brightness and goodness. During our studies at Rome he never had many intimate friends; he was retiring and shunned the common sports and games. His world was around his desk; science and learning were his paradise. He was only twelve or thirteen when I knew him at Viterbo, and yet he wrote Latin prose and verse with marvellous ease and elegance."

In the year 1824, the first dark shadow fell across the life of Vincent: that year he lost his mother. It was a heavy stroke, for the young boy, with his affectionate heart, had loved her passionately. Shortly after his mother's death he went to Rome, where he lived with his uncle, Marquis Muti. There he resumed his classics at the Roman College, under two famous professors of literature, Fathers Ferdinand Menini and Joseph Bonviciui. After completing the course of rhetoric, he studied in the same College philosophy and science under Fathers Carafa, Pianciani and Ferrarini, who in their different branches, were accomplished teachers, as well as authors of great reputation. Pecci was as successful in philosophy as in classics, and though very young he boldly opened his books of theology and attended the lectures of the famous Fathers Perrone, Manera, Patrizi, Zecchinelli, Van Everbroek, Curi and Kohlman. We find in the beautiful Elegy, which he wrote in 1875, a fine tribute of praise to the memories of his old professors. He was a grateful student and knew that much of the pupil's glory belongs to the master.

The future Pontiff was only eighteen when he began to study theology, and at twenty-one was graduated Doctor of Divinity. That he was a deep, mature and able scholar, the *Diary* and *Records* of the old Roman College testify. Think for a moment of that magnificent work. At fifteen, he was leading a large class of rhetoric, at fifteen he had mastered Italian, was a Latinist to the core, and wrote Greek with facility. His taste was universal, and we find him working so hard at science, that he took the first honors for chemistry and physics, and was not far behind in mathematics. His keen intellect and calm reasoning powers made philosophy a delightful study. Honors fell thick upon him, and at the end of three years he was appointed Repetitor in the German College, where only the choicest of the ecclesiastical students of Germany are admitted, after a severe competitive examination.

A perfect classical scholar, a fair scientist, an able philosopher: no wonder, then, that he proved himself so good in theology. And yet it would have been glory enough for the youth of eighteen to have held a place among the lesser lights of that brilliant cluster of students who came from many lands to listen

to the lectures in the Gregorian University. But Pecci was too
ambitious to be satisfied with mediocrity. Day by day his little
star grew larger, till its light shone fairer than the brightest there.
His superiority was openly confessed when he was appointed, at
the end of his third year of theology, to defend all the theses
explained in that year. This was in 1830. The Aula Maxima
was crowded with Cardinals, and prelates, and dignitaries, and all
the great professors of Rome. He had three treatises to explain ;
Indulgences, and the sacraments of Holy Orders and Extreme
Unction. There were three persons appointed beforehand, they
were called in the university *Objectors*, who argued against him and
offered many knotty points for solution. But Pecci was ready to
explain everything. We find in the old *Diary* of the college
words that sound like a prophecy :—"The young man displayed
such ability, that, it would seem, great things are in store for
him."

But Pecci's course was not done; next came Civil and Canon
Law, at the Roman University, *La Sapienza.* Here, from 1831
to 1834, under the care of very able men, particularly of Cardinal Joseph Anthony Sala, whom he loved and prized as a great
scholar, he learned the sound principles of Civil and Canon Law
that now make him illustrious before the world. In 1834, he was
graduated *Doctor Utriusque Juris*, and, at last, at the age of
twenty-four, Vincent Pecci was ready to try in the broad field of
public action his trained arms. The Academy of Noble Ecclesiastics, where he had dwelt these last years, next sent him, as it
usually does with those who have finished their books, for three
years to the Congregations, or Departments of State, of the

Pontifical Curia. There the Catholic Church, in her manifold branches of administration, was unfolded before him; there he read and studied the traditions of the Congregations, with all their wealth of archives to instruct and perfect him; there he found history repeating itself, and questions of the past throwing light upon the present and its conflicts; it was just the work to make a great statesman of him.

But we have not time to tell more of those three years; we hope by this the reader appreciates the splendid training that the Catholic Church gives her princes and rulers. Leo XIII was a student for over twenty years and that, too, with a single aim shaping his whole life. It was this unity that made him a great man. He was never too young to see the bearing of the present on the past and the future. He knew his way in the vast range of mental work that reached from rhetoric to the sublime heights of theology. He was always sure of his ground; he knew where he stood and what would come next. When at last he closed his school books, he could command all that he had ever seen or learned; he was as perfect as education can make a man, and needed only experience to crown the theoretical knowledge of books. Nor had his books made him a dreamer; what he knew of the past, he was able to apply practically to the progress of the present age: he was a citizen of the world, mastering with diverse tongues the best thoughts of all ages. When dignities and offices fell upon him he could bear them gracefully and manfully. Nor can we say that his rapid advance in public trust was due to favoritism or influence. As early as March 16, 1837, he was named Domestic Prelate and Referendary of Both Signatures, whose function it is to procure and dispatch answers to petitions to the Holy See, either for favors or for redress of wrongs. Both these offices are highly prized by Catholic clergymen.

During this year he was ordained sub-deacon and deacon by his Eminence Cardinal Charles Prince Odescalchi, in the chapel of St. Stanislaus Kostka at *Sant' Andrea*, and on the 23d of the following December, in the chapel of the Vicariate of Rome, he was ordained priest. The Golden Jubilee of this event, so fraught with heavenly joy for him, will shortly be celebrated at Rome with befitting pomp and ceremony by the Catholics of the Universal Church. It seems to be the intention of the present rulers of Rome to tear down the first of these two venerated sanctuaries, in order to make room for some public building. But it is to be hoped that the King of Italy will follow the example of his royal father, who on a similar occasion strongly opposed their destruction, and will not allow these sacred monuments of Christian Rome to be demolished.

The deep piety, the quick and ready talent, the profound erudition, the kind and noble manners of the young priest, soon won for him the esteem and affection of the reigning Pontiff, Pope Gregory XVI. He considered Pecci, even at an early age, as worthy and capable of administering the government of the Provinces. When he was but twenty-eight years of age, that is, immediately after his ordination, in 1838, he was appointed Delegate of Benevento, and, subsequently, was advanced with the same title to the government of the larger Delegation of Spoleto and Perugia. In this office he remained only three years, yet, in that short time he gave unmistakable proofs of superior statesmanship and administrative ability.

It may be recollected that rough storms were brewing over the Italian states, when Pecci was entrusted with the management of these important provinces. The tumult of the political hurricane was felt throughout Italy. The revolutionary party, composed of *Young Italy* and the *Carbonari*, had not been unsuccessful in its efforts at revolutionizing the population. That dangerous class which, on such occasions, take advantage of the troubles of the state to come forth from the low and worthless obscurity wherein they lurk for fear of public punishment, attracted the serious attention of Pecci, and with such energy did he pursue them, that in a few months he freed the Province of Benevento from them, and checked effectually all inroads from neighboring banditti. Seven years after he had left this office, I was in Benevento, and I can recall very vividly the marks of gratitude and the terms of praise with which the citizens mentioned the name of Pecci. Indeed, so great was the popularity which he acquired among them by his gentleness and nobility of character, and by the prudence and impartiality of his administration, that, though many excellent men have succeeded him, his absence is felt, and not without regret.

Perugia and Spoleto welcomed him with general satisfaction, when apostolic authority transferred him to that Delegation. An eye witness, the Abbè Brunelli, Professor of the Seminary of Perugia, in an essay read at the Academy of Perugia in September, 1878, sums up, in a few words, the life of Pecci, their Delegate: " In our Perugia, Monsgr. Pecci was not only loved, but, I would almost say, adored. You will remember how from the very beginning he had won the affection of all. It is said that under

his administration, our prisons, so much narrower then than now,
were at one time entirely untenanted. To hope for or even to
fancy such an event at the present time would be sheer folly." It
was in Perugia that, on September 25th, 1841, the Delegate Pecci,
amidst the greatest popular enthusiasm, welcomed Pope Gregory,
who was then visiting the provinces of his temporal states. On
this occasion the Pope could appreciate the merits of Pecci, partly
from the public esteem in which he found him to be held, and
partly from his own intercourse with him on subjects both political
and administrative. Pope Gregory thought that the Holy See
could draw still greater profit from the unusual ability of the
Delegate; so, at the first opportunity, the Holy Father appointed
him, to the deep regret of the people of Perugia and Spoleto,
Nuncio Apostolic to the court of King Leopold I, of Belgium.

On the 19th of February, 1843, Monsgr. Pecci, although not
yet thirty-three years of age, was consecrated, in the church of
San Lorenzo in Panisperna, in Rome, by the famous Cardinal
Luigi Lambruschini, archbishop of Damietta. He arrived in
Brussels on the 8th of April, 1844. The very first day, when
he solemnly presented to the King his papers as Apostolic Nuncio,
his unaffected dignity in word and action won the Royal good will,
and the esteem and confidence of the court. Nor did he by his
subsequent actions belie this first favorable impression. He
abhorred hypocrisy and cunning. His policy consisted chiefly in
speaking the truth without offense and without bitterness to all
alike; to king and courtier, to bishops and faithful. It was here
that he began to inculcate those truths which he has so strongly
and authoritatively maintained since his elevation to the throne

of St. Peter: above all the doctrine that the Catholic Church, instead of hindering civil progress is, on the contrary, its prime mover and most energetic supporter. The principles which we know him to hold to-day, are those which as Nuncio he upheld in Belgium. During this period, he was the very soul, both of the impulses given to, and of the improvements made in, the spiritual and scientific education of the clergy, and in the moral and material welfare of the faithful. He patronized the building of churches, the creation of new institutions of charity, and the foundation or introduction of Religious Orders. He zealously labored to enforce the observance of the Sunday, to bring about a greater reverence and appreciation of the dignity and sacredness of the bond of marriage, and to promote the observance of the sacred rites and ceremonies of our Holy Church.

Nor did his zeal in the performance of his duties check his ardor for self-improvement. He sought a personal acquaintance with the highest dignitaries of the kingdom ; he visited and examined their institutions, especially those founded for the relief of the poor, and he subsequently introduced them into either Perugia or Rome. He obtained an accurate knowledge of the government of the principal cities, and made a study of the oldest and wisest municipal statutes. In a word he became thoroughly conversant with Belgian affairs; and conceived such an affectionate regard for the people that, later, when Bishop of Perugia, he made his own palace the abode of all Belgian visitors and welcomed to it, during their vacations, all the students of the Belgian college at Rome. Following the counsel of wisdom, that the wise man, visiting different countries should observe with care

the good and the evil for his own future advantage, Monsgr.
Pecci, while residing at the court of Leopold, made it his business
when his duties permitted him, to visit the chief cities of the
surrounding countries and thus became acquainted with their
Sovereign Princes and their most eminent prelates, statesmen and
scientists. Thus he visited France, Holland, the Rhine provinces and London. In a word the stay of Pecci in Belgium
proved invaluable to him for the acquisition of that knowledge
of human nature, which has so characterized him since, and has
enabled him to discern the motives of men's action, and to
appreciate the great conflict which sometimes exists between principles and their application. To this period, too, he owes much
of that rare wisdom, prudence and tact, which has of late years so
distinguished his government, as Supreme Head of Christendom.

Meanwhile on April 16, 1845, occurred the death of the vener-
able bishop of Perugia, Monsgr. Carlo Filesio, Marquis Cittadini,
a man of austere and blameless character, of tried experience, the
love and pride of his dear children of Perugia. Mindful of their
beneficent Delegate, and moved by the glory attached to his name,
the devoted Perugians sent an embassy of clerics and laymen to
the Roman Court, urgently requesting the appointment of Pecci
to the vacant see. Though rebuked and dismissed, they were not
disheartened, but so earnestly repeated their request, that they
moved the Holy Father to give his assent. In a consistory held
on the 19th of January, 1846, the last ever held by Gregory,
three years after Pecci's appointment as Nuncio, the important
and exalted charge of the Diocese of Perugia was assigned to him
by the Sovereign Pontiff. The withdrawal of the Nuncio Pecci

was a source of great regret to King Leopold, who esteemed him
so highly and so approved of his measures, that, as a token of his
high regard, he bestowed upon him, by a decree dated May 1,
1846, the Great Cordon of the Royal Order, Saint-Ferdinand,
founded by himself on his accession to the throne of Belgium.

The new bishop made his official entrance into Perugia on the
feast of St. Ann, the 26th of July, 1846. He had chosen this day
in preference to any other, because of his fond affection for his
mother, the Countess Anna, whose presence, indeed, he had lost
some twenty-two years before, but whose deep love and tender
devotedness were ever fresh and lasting in his memory. It is a
singular coincidence and one worth recording, that, at the very
time Monsgr. Pecci was elevated to the see of Perugia, John
Maria Mastai Ferretti ascended the pontifical chair as Supreme
Head of the Church and Vicar of Christ, with the title of Pius
IX. Pecci governed his diocese as long as Pius governed the
Church as Bishop of Rome. Nine years after his elevation to the
bishopric of Perugia, Pius IX created him, in the consistory of
December 17, 1853, a Cardinal of the Holy Roman Church,
under the title of St. Chrysogonus. This event, fraught with
prophetic consequences, added new lustre to his person, and gave
greater celebrity to the see of Perugia.

The see of Perugia, embracing as it does a large population
distributed over an extensive hill-country, is one of the most important dioceses of Italy. The people are of a quick, penetrating
disposition, of sober and industrious habits, and of social manners
which, though simple and manly, evince at once their excellent
mind and refined taste. Their taste and refinement are especially

shown in their appreciation of the nobler arts, an inheritance received from the famous Umbrian school of painting, and carefully preserved to them by the many monuments which have made their churches and other public buildings so deservedly famous. This character, however, is peculiarly befitting Perugia, the chief city of the diocese. As far back as the fourth century before the Christian era, it was known as one of the most powerful cities of Etruria, and, though repeatedly wrecked and burned during the many vicissitudes of war, which it encountered, it has never changed its position from the original lofty hill on which it was founded. To the present day, some of its ancient walls and many singular antiquities attest its remote origin. But with all these memories of a bygone civilization, Perugia now joins the best institutions of modern times. Amongst others, we may mention its University, enjoying a full curriculum of studies from the days of its first establishment in the fifteenth century. The public Library is rich and choice in its various departments and is liberally patronized ; while the Academy of Fine Arts attracts a constant stream of visitors, both of artists in pursuit of their studies and of tourists eager to behold its many celebrated paintings, amongst which are those of the Umbrian school. The churches which adorn the city are not less a source of interest and admiration : splendid in their architectural beauties without, and impressive and captivating by their wealth of magnificent sculpture and exquisite painting within ; while its numerous and flourishing institutions of education and charity display the practical and energetic spirit of the people of Perugia.

We can readily imagine that the Episcopal care of such a population was by no means a light one, since, as has been so well

said, the difficulty of ruling a people is in direct proportion to
their degree of culture. It was, however, the glory of Bishop
Pecci to govern this diocese for thirty-two years to the great satisfaction of all its varied classes, and not only to have preserved the
advantages of which he found it possessed, but to have greatly
improved its existing institutions and to have introduced many
others. In such a sketch of his life as the present, it would be
impossible to enter into the details of his Episcopal administration,
and we must content ourselves with striving to present merely a
general outline of what he accomplished and of the means which
he was so careful to employ in every department of labor.

The great secret of Bishop Pecci's activity lies in the plan of
life which he adopted at his first entrance on the see of Perugia.
Though of a slender frame and delicate health, he never allowed
himself any of the indulgences or useless comforts of life. He
rose early every morning, daybreak always finding him on his
knees in prayer, while in every season of the year he made it his
custom to retire at ten o'clock. He took but one meal a day, and
that of the simplest and most frugal kind. He never indulged
in idle or useless conversations, and his different walks and journeys
were taken when necessity or charity demanded them. Never,
therefore, losing a moment of time, he was able to double his
natural activity and greatly multiply his labors. When others
who assisted him, or who commenced their work after he had begun, would feel fatigued, he himself was still fresh and vigorous.
It was in this way that he always found leisure, not only for the
reception of his numerous visitors and the speedy dispatch of his
daily routine of office, but also for extensive study, meditation and

writing on the great discoveries and problems of the day. Pursuing such a life of regularity and labor, it is not surprising that he was able to undertake so many various works and bestow his personal care upon them all, even to the smallest particulars.

His principal solicitude, however, was for the clergy of his diocese. He found them, indeed, a learned, pious and zealous body, and some superiors would doubtless have been satisfied with the moderate care of preserving them in this commendable condition; but Bishop Pecci aimed at a loftier standard of perfection. He began his course of improvements at the very root of the matter, the first education, namely, of the young candidates for the priesthood. During the earliest years of his episcopate, he practically rebuilt the diocesan seminary, making it roomier, healthier, better arranged for purposes of discipline, and more amply furnished with the accommodations required for a higher course of literary, philosophical and theological studies. To enlarge the seminary, he did not hesitate even to sacrifice a part of his episcopal residence. He then improved the entire program of studies by arranging them in a more methodical order and adding several new branches to the course. He made it a special care to select as professors men of the greatest talent and learning, and spared no means in his power to excite their zeal in the service of the seminary. He often assisted at their lectures; he praised them publicly and rewarded them handsomely, according to their merits: while at the same time he never failed to admonish them in the kindest and gentlest manner of their little deficiencies.

One of the professors relates a story in point, which shows us how sweetly these admonitions were often conveyed. At the time of the occurrence, Bishop Pecci had been raised to the dignity of Cardinal. One day the professor, for some reason or another, came to his class-room a few moments after the appointed time. What was his astonishment on entering to behold the Cardinal himself seated in his chair, explaining a passage in the Oration for Milo! The Cardinal stopped his explanation at once, and warmly exhorted the students to continue with increased earnestness their study of the classics. He then saluted the professor kindly and withdrew. We might wonder how the Cardinal could have known of this delay of only a few moments, but as the professor perceived, it could not have happened except through the personal vigilance which he employed over the discipline and studies of the house. He was accustomed to come almost daily to the seminary, which was close to the Palace, and to spend an hour or two in careful scrutiny of its workings. At times he listened to the lectures of the professors, and at times to the repetitions of the students. He always presided at every examination or public act of the students. He was also, we must add, equally solicitous for their bodily comfort, and kept himself well informed of how the seminarians were treated in this respect, especially when he found that any of them were indisposed or seriously ill.

It was in this seminary that he first introduced the Academy of St. Thomas, to promote the study of the Angelic Doctor's philosophical and theological principles. His interest, however, for the welfare of the seminary was never better displayed than when by the Italian Government's confiscation laws the seminary had been crippled in its revenues. The Cardinal immediately undertook its support from his own personal revenues. His greatest

recompense, and one which was dearest to his heart, was the happy
fruit which he gathered from so many cares and sacrifices; for the
clergy of Perugia became one of the most learned and edifying
bodies in all Italy.

While thus attending to the education of the younger clergy,
Cardinal Pecci was not less vigilant for the safety and prosperity
of the priests who were actively engaged in the different spheres
of the ministry. He followed the steps of each of them with a
more paternal anxiety. The impressive thought of his own great
responsibility as well as theirs, kept him constantly engaged in
securing the most appropriate means for the welfare, not only of
the whole body, but of every individual. He began his labor in
this direction by publishing, in 1851, a decree concerning the discipline of the clergy, which he afterwards scrupulously enforced
throughout his administration. In 1856 he addressed all the parish
priests in a Pastoral on the duty of teaching the Christian doctrine
and the best means of complying therewith. In the following year
he addressed them in a second Pastoral, in which he laid down a
common method of discipline for the observance of all in the
direction of their parishes. He gave them besides many more
particular instructions on their manifold obligations, amongst
which we may mention the Rules he prescribed in 1866, for their
conduct during times of political commotion. They were remarkable for their wisdom and prudence, and are still looked upon as
a masterly system of guidance in such difficult emergencies.

The means which he employed to keep himself constantly and
accurately informed concerning the conduct of his clergy, were
chiefly two. The first was the free and ever ready access to him-

self, which was always marked by a kind reception and generous hospitality. The other was the regular visitation which he made of all the parishes, churches, and pious institutions of the Diocese, a duty which is prescribed by canon law as of the highest importance. During his term of office as Bishop, he made this visitation seven times. He was unable, however, to complete the last, owing to his being called to Rome to assume the exalted dignity of Camerlengo of the Roman Church, which had been left vacant by the death of Cardinal de Angelis. Nor was his care for his clergy confined to their spiritual improvement, but it extended equally to their temporal welfare. He showed himself a magnanimous as well as a tender father, and none of his clergy ever required his help without immediately receiving it, even before they made their necessities known. When the iniquitous law imposing the compulsory enrolment of all young Italians in the military service rendered the priesthood liable to the draft, he founded the pious work called the *Exemption of Clergymen from Actual Service*, by which those of the clergy who might be called upon to enter the army should be assisted in freeing themselves by paying the government a heavy tax. Another of his foundations was the *Consorzio* of St. Joachim for ecclesiastics, where those of the clergy who, by illness, old age, or any other inability, needed support, could find it in a manner becoming their station.

His zeal for the worship of God was likewise as great as it was enlightened. As this is the one supreme end to which the Divine institution of the Church is directed, so it was the object of his constant watchfulness. Whatever could in any way foster the piety of his flock, he embraced with joy. More than thirty

new churches were erected during his episcopate, and as many
others were restored and improved. The Cathedral Church
especially was adorned with costly marbles and paintings and
enriched with precious vestments and golden vases. The usual
services in the churches and the ordinary practices of piety he
caused to be elevated to a nobler standard. He never failed to
assist at them personally, and enhanced the effect of the sacred
ceremonies by performing them with the most solemn rites. He
frequently addressed the people with exhortations and sacred
homilies, in which his natural eloquence and profound learning
gave such strength and persuasion to his words, that they never
failed to produce salutary effects. Some of these exhortations
were afterwards printed for the benefit of the whole diocese, and
were found to be models of sacred oratory as well as evident
proofs of a truly episcopal zeal. Besides these oral addresses,
he was also accustomed to issue frequent Pastoral Letters for
the edification and instruction of all his people. Scarcely a
year passed without the publication of one or two of them.
They treated with unusual breadth and thoroughness the most
important topics of the day, such, for example, as the abuse of
magnetism; the temporal dominion of the Pope; the impious
work of Rénan, *The life of Jesus Christ*; the current errors and
prejudices in matters of religion; the tendency of the present day
to deny Revelation; the Catholic Church and the nineteenth
century; the relations between the Church and civilization; and
many similar subjects, befitting both the times and the flock committed to his charge.

With all these cares, Bishop Pecci was not less zealous for
the secular instruction and material relief of his subjects. The

University of Perugia, of which he was *ex-officio* the Grand Chan-
cellor, he reformed in various ways. He also founded many
colleges for the instruction of boys, and seminaries for the higher
education of girls. For the children of the poor, he founded and
widely spread what he called the *Gardens of St. Philip Neri*,
where the children could spend their Sundays in religious worship
and the hearing of useful instruction and in innocent amusements.
There were none of the pious institutions for the relief of the needy,
into which he did not introduce great and wholesome changes.
Others, such as the *Orphan Asylum* for women suffering from
chronic diseases, he himself founded and endowed.

A natural consequence of all this solicitude was the way in which
it endeared him to all his people. Their affection was shown in a
very loving way in 1869, when he celebrated the Silver Jubilee
of his Episcopate. The demonstrations of joy and gratitude on
the part of all classes of the people were sincere and tender beyond
expression, and he himself declared that they surpassed his greatest expectations, and were the best human reward he could desire
for his labors in behalf of his flock.

This rapid enumeration of some of the facts of his episcopal life
may give some idea of the zeal and nobility of mind and heart,
with which Cardinal Pecci adorned the Bishopric of Perugia. It
may be added that during his administration there, he found himself involved in the storms of three successive revolutions: that of
1848–49, which lasted almost a year; that of 1859, which was of
short duration and ended with the taking of Perugia by the Pontifical troops, so much calumniated for the act; and, lastly, that
of the autumn of 1860, when the Piedmontese army invaded the

States of the Pope. In each of these revolutions, Cardinal Pecci
had much to suffer, but throughout he was ever true to his lofty
character: charitable, firm, cautious and prudent; so that he was
able to inspire the hearts of the very enemies of the priesthood and
of the Roman purple with a sense of reverence for himself and his
sacred office. A proof of this was given in 1861, when Perugia
had fallen into the hands of the Piedmontese. Three of his priests
had provoked him to suspend them from their sacerdotal functions,
because of their scandalous cooperation with the revolutionists.
They then insolently summoned him before the tribunal of Perugia, in the hope of their being supported by the civil power in
whose favor they had acted. The court, however, respected the
rights of the Cardinal and allowed him full liberty over his refrac-
tory clergy.

As we have said, Pius IX, in a consistory held on the 21st of September, 1877, appointed Cardinal Pecci to the office of Camerlengo
of the Church. He was accordingly called to Rome to enter upon
the exercise of his new duties. The event proved that this appointment was part of the plan of Divine Providence in his regard.
For, thus it was brought about that Cardinal Pecci became a per-
manent resident of Rome, shortly before the death of the admirable Pontiff he was destined so worthily to succeed.

The Cardinal Camerlengo, at the death of a Pope, is invested
with the highest powers for the administration of the Church, till
the election of a new Pope; and on him especially rests the
responsible duty of preparing the Conclave for the nomination of
a successor to the chair of St. Peter. On February 7th, 1878,
Pius IX, having outlived the reign of the Prince of the Apostles,

went to receive the well won recompense of his saintly life and
faithful stewardship. When the solemn obsequies were over, the
Conclave was opened on the 18th of February, four months and
a half after the arrival in Rome of Cardinal Pecci. In the
Sacred College of Cardinals there was no doubt as to who was best
fitted both in wisdom and grace to succeed Pius IX. Remarkable
alike for virtue and learning, Cardinal Pecci gained at once the
suffrages of the august electors. On February 20th, 1878, after
thirty-six hours of conclave, he was elected Sovereign Pontiff to
the joy of all Christendom; and accepting, though with great
reluctance, the high dignity thus conferred upon him, he took the
name of Leo XIII.

The newly-elected Pope was an Italian by birth, and a citizen
of the States of the Church. During the thirty-two years of his
residence in Perugia he had shown himself a holy and zealous
Bishop. And this fidelity in so important a charge, accompanied
as it was by a large experience in the transactions of diplomatic
and administrative affairs, was sufficient warrant of his worth. To
these two qualities was added great learning in theology, canon
law, philosophy, and all branches of classic literature. He was
already in the sixty-eighth year of his age: and thus what is
usually a time of rest for others, was for him but the beginning of
a life of wonderful activity. Though his delicate health, impaired
by past labors, might have justified in him an old age of repose,
yet he addressed himself to his lofty task with an energy that
never slackened. A strong mind and generous heart can often
give vigor to a failing body. Though the field of Leo's work was
by his elevation so widely extended, and his responsibility before

God and man so greatly increased, he found in his mind and heart
virtue, powerful enough to make up for bodily weakness.

No Roman Pontiff ever ascended the throne in more critical
circumstances. He was the successor of one who for many years
had been a prisoner in the Papal Palace. Pius IX had won from
the Catholic world the title of Great, which was but the just
reward of his high virtues, his heroic endurance, and his never
failing benevolence. Leo XIII was to succeed Pius IX, not
only as the warder of God's Church on earth, but also as the
Prisoner in the Vatican, and as the cherished Father of the faithful. He found the temporal power of the Holy See usurped, the
necessary instruments of administration impaired, and a tendency
in almost all the secular powers of Europe to lessen or even to
destroy the rights of the Catholic Church. Great were the expectations that attended the opening of Leo's reign; but the difficulties that surrounded him were even greater. A cursory glance
at the first eight years will show how freely Leo XIII has answered
those hopes by overcoming the causes that combined to darken
and hinder their fulfilment.

No one can fail to see how Leo XIII has exerted himself to forward the spirit of piety and religion By three successive jubilees
he has brought down manifold blessings on his enterprises, and
amongst those blessings that greatest of all, the reform of Christian
life throughout the whole world. To foster this reform and to
increase it, he has raised to the honor of the altar many a hero of
saintliness. Thus the faithful have not only been led to higher
perfection, but are encouraged to persevere therein after the pat-
tern of exalted models. It was in order to stimulate the spirit of

charity towards the indigent and suffering that he proposed as
Patron of all pious works the great St. Vincent de Paul ; while to
those engaged in pursuit of philosophical and theological studies,
he has given as a model and protector, St. Thomas of *Aquino*, the
Angel of the Schools. A powerful aid to the amendment of life
and the defence of virtue in secular persons was his exhortation to
all the faithful to join the Third Order of St. Francis, whose members take a special pledge, under the patronage of St. Francis of
Assisi, to keep the commandments of God and the precepts of the
Church as faithfully as possible. As for devotion to the Blessed
Mother of God, who does not know of the advancement it has
received from the filial love of Her Son's Representative ? Not
content with ordering prayers to be said in her honor at the end
of every Mass, he has consecrated the month of October to her,
under the title of Queen of the Most Holy Rosary. In fact, we
can safely assert that scarcely a month of these eight years has
not been characterized by some means or other employed by His
Holiness to spread and strengthen devotion.

But his most thoughtful care has been given to the Episcopal
Hierarchy of the Church. Never has he in the choice of Pastors
of the flock of Christ sacrificed the Church's interest to gratify the
caprices of the princes of the world. His selections of Bishops
have been always most judicious ; and this too in accordance with
existing laws and concordats. At times he has not hesitated to
modify such customs and conventions, in order to secure a more
successful result. One of the first acts of his Pontificate, in 1878,
was to appoint a commission of five Cardinals, who were to select
with care and discretion such Italian priests as were worthiest of

the mitre. Nor has his care in the choice of clergymen extended
only over Italy and the other European nations; but here, in the
United States of America, we have felt that his acquaintance with
our needs was that of one who lived among us.

Coming to that highest dignity which it is in the Pope's power
to confer, we see that Leo's prudence has shone especially where
prudence in the choice of prelates ought chiefly to be manifested;
for it is with the August College of Cardinals that the Pope has
to consult in affairs of administration, and in the solution of
whatever difficult questions may occur. Leo XIII has already
held eight consistories for the creation of Cardinals; of those
raised by His Holiness to the Cardinalate, thirty-six are still
living: and it may in truth be said that they form a constellation,
which the Catholics of any age might be proud to own and
venerate. Their names are too familiar to the world to call for
any notice here. Newman is amongst them, and Hergenröther,
and Zigliara, and Pecci, and Alimonda, and Lavigerie, and
Capecelatro, and Mazzella, and our own beloved James Gibbons,
Cardinal Archbishop of Baltimore.

The constitution of the different national hierarchies has been
another zealous care of the Holy Father. By successive Bulls
he has established new Hierarchies and created new Sees. The
countries thus benefitted were Scotland, Poland, Bosnia, Herze-
govina; as well as North and South America, together with Asia,
Africa and Oceania. He put an end to the schism of Armenia,
and received at the Vatican with the greatest kindness the bishops
and priests who had been the originators and warmest supporters
of the schism. Besides the ordinary visits *ad Límina*, during which

every Bishop is personally bound to give to the Pope an account
of his diocesan administration, Pope Leo XIII, has frequently
summoned to Rome the more eminent prelates of different countries, that they might with greater facility and freedom make
known their wants, and receive in return the assistance of His
Holiness, along with his counsel and direction. The memory
shall long remain of that time, when the American Archbishops
and Bishops gathered in Rome in preparation for the Third
Plenary Council of Baltimore. The kind reception they met with
at the hands of the Pope was such, as the Vicar of Christ alone
could give.

Nor has a warm and open welcome been the only consolation
given by Leo XIII to the Prelates who have gone to him in behalf
of the churches committed to their charge. In every hardship
and difficulty, the whole Hierarchy of the Church have found in
him a constant helper and an unerring adviser ; while his letters
addressed to them at various times have been marked as well by
nobility of style, as by elevation of thought and the wisdom of the
teaching. It is saying but little to assert that they will long out-
live the false maxims they refute and the evils they condemn. Who
does not remember the eloquent Encyclical, addressed to the Italian
Bishops in 1882 ? In it they are earnestly exhorted to defend the
Christian Faith against sectarian attacks, against an ungodly press,
and against the teachings of infidel professors. Later on when
Catholicity in Holland was threatened by revolutionary societies,
aiming at the destruction of authority and morality, His Holiness
addressed to the Bishops of that country letters full of instruction
and encouragement. With like wise vigilance has he directed

his eyes towards the struggle, carried forward by the Catholics
of Spain against impiety, immorality, and oppression. His Encyclical sent at that depressing time to the Spanish Bishops is marked
throughout by the tender sympathy and the far-seeing wisdom of
a Father and a Ruler. Nor was his powerful influence unfelt,
nor his pacifying voice unheeded by the Bishops of Milan, Turin,
and Vercelli, during the bitter quarrel in which the Catholic jour-
nals of these cities stood opposed to one another on mere questions
of science. Such in a few words have been the Encyclicals of
Leo XIII. They are stamped in every instance with the impress
of his own exalted mind. It is astonishing how, notwithstanding
the manifold and distracting cares of his Pontificate, Our Holy
Father has found time to write these Encyclicals. Though every
year has called for some letters from Leo XIII, those to which we
have referred were all written during the year 1882, alone.

Nor did the Holy Father cease here to wield his pen for the
consolation and advancement of his children. Besides these
special communications to different countries, he has, on several
occasions of more universal importance, addressed Encyclical
Letters to all the Bishops of the Church. These Encyclicals are
splendid specimens of forcible eloquence, and living monuments
of wisdom and learning. In them the Christian world recognizes
that elevation of thought, that nobility of mind and that refinement of culture, which are on all sides acknowledged to belong
to the present Pontiff. As the space allotted to this biography
is necessarily limited, we must content ourselves with a simple
enumeration of the topics that form their subject matter. This
brief summary will, however, satisfactorily demonstrate how oppor-

tune and how well suited to the needs of our time are the counsels
of our provident Father.

His first Encyclical which treats of Progress, is dated April 21,
1878. In it Pope Leo proves, in his own masterly way, that the
Church, far from being the enemy of Progress, has ever been and
will continue to be the zealous promoter of that humanizing
civilization and social culture, which are everywhere esteemed
the very consummation of Progress. Towards the end of the
same year, on December 28, he gave to the world another Encyclical, which may be with propriety styled the complement of its
predecessor. It is a magnificent and a sweeping refutation and
condemnation of Socialism, Communism, and Nihilism. Under
the skilful hand of Leo XIII, their sophistries are unmasked and
their doctrines made to appear in all their native hideousness.
Every honest man, that peruses this letter with any attention, cannot but agree with its learned and authoritative teaching, that
Socialism, Communism, and Nihilism are alike subversive of the
Gospel and of civil society, and that they are as insuperable
hindrances to the prosperity of the State, as they are to the benig-
nant influence of Christian morality.

The sanctity of Matrimony so seriously threatened in our days
by short-sighted legislators, is placed in clear light, and defended
by Pope Leo in his Encyclical of February 10, 1880. He bases
all his remarks on the primitive institution of marriage by God
Himself in the garden of Eden, and on the elevation of wedlock
to the dignity of a Sacrament in the New Law, promulgated by
Our Lord Jesus Christ. In this Encyclical he evinces his steadfast adherence to the traditions of the Holy See. The Roman

Pontiffs rather than yield a tittle to the concupiscences of men
in this vitally important point, have braved the might and the
anger of emperors and kings.

In the following year, June 21, 1881, he again adverted to the
social and political troubles that agitate the world. He penned
from an evangelical standpoint an elaborate defence of that
authority which is the life-giving principle of all governments,
whatever their form, and whatever their origin. God, he there
shows conclusively, and God alone, vests ruler and people with
their peculiar rights, and imposes on them their reciprocal duties.
But of all Pope Leo's Encyclicals none made a deeper impression
on the world of thought, none evoked more widespread interest,
than his *Immortale Dei*, published November 1, 1885. Here,
as the universal teacher of the Church, he lays down and eluci-
dates the principles, which must actuate every body of men,
ambitious of the name of government; principles, which spring
from the very nature of society, and, therefore, from the designs
and ideas of God Himself. Apart from the teacher's high
authority, which lends so great a weight to this exposition, all
agree that, on this particular subject, the Encyclical in compre-
hensiveness, depth and moderation of tone is unequalled.

The Sovereign Pontiff, as beseems his high office, ever yearns
with all the solicitude of a father for the wellbeing of the Missions. Nor is this solicitude misplaced. For the Missions are
outposts that do battle with error, and plant the Standard of the
Cross in the enemy's country. They slowly and silently subjugate
whole nations, and reduce peoples to the mild sway of the Gospel.
What interest should be closer to the heart of Christ's Vicar than

the propagation of Christ's name and the spread of His Empire!
In Leo XIII, this zeal has been notably active and fruitful. To
set this statement of ours in bolder relief, we need only cursorily
glance at the favors he has heaped on the different Missions, and
thence image to ourselves the paternal anxiety with which he
guards their interests.

We prefer to speak first of the kindness that the Missions in
general have experienced at his hands. On December 3d, 1880,
at the very beginning of his Pontificate, he addressed to the Catholic Episcopacy his splendid Encyclical, *Sancta Dei Civitas*.
In it he urges the piety and the charity of all Christendom to
assist with prayers and with alms the work of the Missions.
Descending to particulars, he mentions as especially worthy of
thoughtful concern the Propaganda, the Holy Childhood, and the
Eastern Schools. The Congregation of the Propaganda and of
the Oriental Rites, to which are entrusted the welfare and enlight-
enment of almost innumerable Christian Communities, spread over
the surface of the earth, has claimed the present Pontiff's most
earnest attention. To strengthen this Congregation and to render it
equal to its task, he has appointed to it Cardinals and Prelates distinguished alike for their rare talents and their long experience.
When the Italian Government dared to execute what neither former
revolutionists, nor the French invaders of Rome under Napoleon
I, were bold enough to carry into effect, viz., the confiscation of
the land property belonging to the Congregation, and devoted to
the support of Missionaries and Missions; Leo XIII, after having
in vain tried by all means to avert so disastrous a calamity, after
having loudly protested against the injustice of the measure, pro-

vided for the future security of the Congregation by removing the administration of its revenues out of Italy. Unhappy times, when the propagation of our Holy Faith is exposed to the unhallowed touch of the usurper's hand in the very capital of Christianity!

Missionary priests, both regular and secular, should be, to use the admirable words of our Lord Jesus Christ, the salt and the light of the earth. Mindful of this, Leo has by wise and salutary regulations provided them with most abundant helps. They are, first, to master by special and energetic study the Eastern tongues: then, to add to a plentiful store of sacred learning a deep knowledge of the natural sciences; and, last of all, while abroad they are to devote the time, free from active missionary duties, to the collection of documents and memorials, that may in any way serve to illustrate the geography, the natural history, the traditions and, especially, the religions of each country.

With regard to the different missions in particular, we may mention the Delegates whom Leo XIII sent with letters and costly presents to the Shah of Persia and to the three Emperors of Turkey, China and Japan, to assure them of the loyalty of their Christian subjects, and to commend these same subjects to their Majesties' protection. From each of them the Pope received most kind and courteous answers, accompanied with promises the most explicit, that the Christians of their respective dominions should enjoy the same privileges and the same liberty as their other subjects. Facts proved afterwards, to the great advantage of the Missions, the sincerity of these promises. We have elsewhere spoken of the happy termination of the Armenian schism. He crowned this event by

raising to the Cardinalate their Patriarch, Mgr. Hassoun, the valiant champion of Catholic unity. To bind closer together the
Missions and Vicariates of India, and to facilitate communication
with the Propaganda, he created two Apostolic Delegates, one for
Oriental India, the other in the Punjub for British India. In the
United States of North America he raised the Bishopric of Chicago
to an Archdiocese, and erected the new Dioceses of Kansas City,
Davenport, Trenton, Grand Rapids, Helena and Manchester, and
the new Vicariate of Dakota. In Canada the new Diocese of Chi-
coutimi and Peterborough owe their establishment to the present
Pontiff. The Apostolic Vicariate at Pontiac and the Prefecture
of the Gulf of St. Lawrence are also creations of his. Besides the
Apostolic Delegates deputed to Hayti and several Republics of
South America, a new Archbishop was named for San Domingo.
The Salesian Fathers, through the impulse and under the direction of Leo XIII, are laboring successfully in Patagonia. Even
Oceanica, whither new bands of missionaries have already been
dispatched, begins to experience the all-pervading influence of his
universal zeal. A small party of these missionaries, landing on the
coast of New Guinea, gave to it the name of Port Leo.

The Catholic Hierarchy of Australia has been honored by the
elevation of the Archbishop of Sidney to the Cardinalate. Its
first National Council marks the beginning of a new era of
activity and prosperity in that country. Africa, too, has come
in for its share of the Pontiff's solicitude. Monsgr. Massaia, the
indefatigable apostle of the Gallas, has been raised by him to the
dignity of the Roman Purple. He has restored the ancient
Metropolitan See of Carthage. Apostolic Delegates have been

sent by him to Victoria Nyanza, to the Island of Madagascar, and to Zanguibar. During his reign, likewise, the Apostolic Prefectures of the Gold Coast, Dahomey and Zambeze have been established. This hurried mention of scattered facts is, we presume, evidence enough of the zealous care, with which Leo provides for distant laborers in the Lord's vineyard, and of the impetus and vigor that nine years of energy and zeal have infused into the work of the Missions.

Among the many qualifications which led the Cardinal electors to make choice of the Bishop of Perugia for the Roman Pontificate, none better fitted him for that high office, in those turbulent times, than his eminent political abilities, of which more than once he had furnished abundant proofs. At the time of his election the relations existing between the Holy See and the Sovereign States of Europe placed the occupant of the Pontifical Throne in a peculiarly trying position. The government of Italy, not satisfied with having deprived the Holy See of its temporal possessions, sought also to fetter the personal liberty of the Pontiff. Prussia and Russia were threatening to cut off from their Catholic subjects all intercourse with their Supreme Pastor at Rome. France and Belgium were ruled by unbelievers who were endeavoring to eradicate the principles, which Christianity had implanted in the hearts of the people. Nor was the condition of affairs in the other States of Europe more assuring. If hostilities were fewer and enmity less apparent, still, instances were not wanting in which the rights of the Church were disregarded, and even, at times, openly violated. Not the least arduous, therefore, of the duties of the new Pope, was the task of quieting these

animosities and introducing better feelings between the Powers of
Europe and the Church over which he ruled.

To this duty Leo XIII applied himself with characteristic
vigor. No sooner had he been elevated to the chair of St. Peter,
than he began this laborious work; and with a wisdom, prudence
and perseverance, which few could better exert; by an admirable
selection of the means and a delicate tact in applying them; he
has, in a few years, achieved greater success, than even his most
sanguine hopes could have led him to expect. Many and great
are the changes which have been brought about by his untiring
zeal. With Prince Nikita a concordat has been entered into, which
secures the diocesan independence of the Principalities of Monte-
negro. A treaty between the Holy See and the Canton of *Ticino*
has settled many long standing troubles, relating to Episcopal
jurisdiction. The king of Belgium again sends his minister
to the Pontifical Court. Portugal, too, recognizes the influence
of the Vatican. Negotiations for a new concordat were opened on
the very day that the Prince of Portugal celebrated his nuptials.
In Spain more freedom is given to the bishops and clergy in the
exercise of their respective duties, and some of the most obnoxious
laws have been ameliorated, or practically abolished. In recog-
nition of these favors the Pope, in 1886, presented the Golden
Rose to Her Catholic Majesty, the Queen Regent. With Austria
the relations have been most friendly; and on the occasion of the
marriage of the Archduke in 1881, the Pope showed his kindly
feelings by sending rich presents to the Imperial couple. In
France, owing to the aggressive policy of the party in power, the
influence of His Holiness has been less effectual, and his efforts have

met with less success; but even here much has been gained, as
was lately proved by the amicable adjustment of the difficulties
relating to the diplomatic representation in China.

With the Italian Government, quite a different course of action
had to be pursued. Here there was no room for reconciliation.
Not only do the interests of the Catholic world and the sacred
dignity of the Vicar of Christ require the Pope to protect the
rights and possessions of the Holy See, but he is bound moreover,
by his oath of office, to defend them, if necessary, even with his
blood. These rights and possessions the Italian Government has
usurped and still retains. Nor is it the intention of the present
rulers of Italy to restore the least portion of what they have so
unjustly seized. True, they ask for a reconciliation with the
Holy See; but for what purpose? Is it not to obtain a kind of
absolution for past offenses, and to secure for the future a sort of
right to enjoy their unlawful conquests in peace? What could
Leo XIII do in such circumstances? He had no choice but to
follow in the footsteps of his predecessor, Pius IX. Again and
again has he fearlessly renewed the same protestations, asserted
the same rights, brought forward the same complaint.

This he must do; but mark the moderation and meekness which
characterizes his every act in this unpleasant duty. In not one of
his writings on this subject is there found a single expression which
could be made to convey a feeling of bitterness, much less a desire
for revenge. On the contrary, the unprejudiced reader finds in them
the sentiments of a man who has as much at heart the welfare and
glory of Italy, as the advancement and triumph of religion or the
protection and prosperity of the Church of God. And this course

of action on the part of His Holiness is gradually producing a change in the minds of the most eminent statesmen, many of whom do not hesitate to predict a revival, for the near future, of the Roman Question, and what is more important, its speedy solution in accordance with the principles of truth and justice.

So far we have passed in review the Catholic states of Europe, and remarked the success which attended the efforts of Leo in his dealings with them. A like success, and, indeed a more striking one, if we consider the circumstances, followed his endeavors with the three non-Catholic states of Europe : England, Russia and Prussia. So anxious was England to enter into diplomatic relations with the Holy See, that, in 1884, she sent a resident agent to the Eternal City, who, though not possessing any official authority, was there to await a time, when favorable circumstances would permit of his appointment as resident Minister at the Vatican. Pius IX, after many negotiations with Russia, was doomed to disappointment, and failed to obtain any satisfactory result. More success has attended the efforts of his successor. In 1880 preliminary negotiations were opened between the Czar and the Pope. Two years later a concordat was signed, which allowed the exiled Bishops of Poland to return from their Siberian prisons ; the present Hierarchy was established ; freedom was again granted to the Catholic Poles, and a day of peace and prosperity began to dawn upon the patient, much tried and suffering church of Poland.

But greater patience and more delicate tact were required on the part of the Pope in his dealings with the German Empire: and here too the wise conduct of Leo won the day. Immediately upon his accession to the Pontifical throne, he sent an urgent request to the Emperor William, asking a repeal, or, at least, a mitigation of those famous laws against the Catholics of Germany. He took occasion at the same time to draw the attention of the Emperor to the past conduct of those subjects of His Majesty: praising their loyalty and patriotism, and assuring him of their continued fidelity. Nor did he remain satisfied with this one appeal, but continued to reiterate his demand for justice until, in 1882, the government took it into serious consideration. From this resulted, in the following year, a modification by the Landtag, of these most obnoxious laws, and a more favorable interpretation, with less rigid enforcement, of those remaining unchanged. Besides this, the Catholic Church is daily growing in favor with German statesmen, so that we may hope soon to see those odious laws repealed, and full liberty granted once more to the bishops and pastors in the exercise of their duties.

These happy results and encouraging prospects are the fruits of the wisdom, tact and talent, joined to the conciliatory spirit of Leo XIII. The world at large pays homage to his abilities. The greatest statesman of the day has given remarkable evidence of his appreciation of them. Germany had taken possession of one of the Caroline Islands, which was claimed by Spain as part of her dominions. Each nation considered her honor and interest at stake. No amicable settlement could be made. Diplomatic negotiations proved fruitless. The situation grew, daily, more complicated, and at one moment war between the two nations seemed imminent. In this crisis Prince Bismarck bethought himself of the Pope, and proposed him as arbiter in the dispute. The proposal was accepted by Spain: and Leo XIII, after mature con-

sideration, issued his *Proposal of Arbitration*, in which he so well
reconciled the claims of both parties to the demands of justice,
that his verdict was gladly accepted, and harmony restored. Thus
was one of the Prerogatives of the Vicar of the Prince of Peace,
Arbiter of Nations, recognized in the reigning Pontiff, and exer-
cised by him, as of old by his illustrious predecessors, recognized
too by a Protestant government in the full tide of its material
and military progress.

Our sketch would be incomplete were we to leave unnoticed
another feature in the character of Leo XIII, his love of learning.
This he has evinced by the efforts he has made to promote the arts
and sciences, and by the favor he has shown their votaries. From
all nations he has called to positions of dignity, to the Cardinalate,
and to the highest offices of the Roman Curia, men distinguished
no less for profound piety than for high culture. What he has
done to foster sacred and philosophical learning, and to promote
among clergy and laity a high standard of culture, we can, in the
limits of our sketch, touch upon but lightly.

He first directed his attention to the interests of philosophy
in Catholic schools, and particularly in Theological Seminaries.
But a few months after his elevation to the Papal Throne, he
issued his famous Encyclical, *Aeterni Patris*, in which he directed
that the system of St. Thomas of *Aquino* be made the groundwork
of all philosophical teaching; and adding practice to precept, he
immediately proceeded to introduce into all the Roman Colleges
and Seminaries under his care the system of teaching he had just
laid down. Nor did he stop here. He called to Rome the
ablest professors of theology and metaphysics. He founded a

Pontifical Academy for the study and propagation of the doctrines of St. Thomas, and caused a new edition of the Angelic
Doctor's works to be printed, sparing no pains to ensure whatever critical ability and diligent examination could add to its
accuracy. He established, moreover, funds for an annual gold
medal to be awarded to the most successful competitor on subjects
within the scope of the Academy ; and he ordered that the transactions of the society be printed and distributed freely among
the Seminaries of Italy. He also ordained that extraordinary
disputations in metaphysics be held at the Vatican itself by
various Universities in the Eternal City ; on all which occasions
he himself, however burdened with care, never fails to lend his
interest and his presence. He has also instituted at Rome a
special school to form thorough professors of philosophy. His
authority, persuasion, and example have not failed of their effect.
As a unit, the Catholic world has followed up the movement
which he so happily inaugurated ; and the traditions of the
Fathers with the teachings of the Doctors now form the solid
foundation, on which is erected the edifice of Catholic thought.

Nor has he slighted the claims of History. The advancement
of this study, he has entrusted to three Cardinals of marked
ability—Hergenröther, Parocchi and Bartolini. Out of more
than four thousand large volumes of the *Regesta* (hitherto sealed
to the public), these princes of the Church are to gather, and lay
before the world all the authentic acts, decrees, and official papers
of the Popes, and the reports of their Legates. Further, they
are to publish critical studies of these documents in historical
works, and to continue down to our own times the History of the

Church, so excellently begun by Baronius and Raynaldi, and that they may not fail to carry out these ambitious plans, the Pope has appointed, as collaborators with these three Cardinals, many able scholars. But the plans of His Holiness embrace a still wider field. All historical students have now free access to these archives: and already several governments, availing themselves of this permission, have sent to Rome representative historians, to gather material for their national histories. To bring these documents within the reach of all, Leo has established a Chair of Paleography, and has called expressly to Rome, the celebrated Canon de Calini to assume its professorship. Many invaluable works have already been published; still more are in preparation, and it is not rash to conjecture that these documents will throw a new light upon profane as well as ecclesiastical annals, and that many a trite and bitter calumny against the Church, will be wiped from the pages of history forever.

These plans, however, have not caused the Holy Father to lose sight of classical literature. Himself an accomplished litterateur, he wishes the Catholic world to attain to that culture, which the languages are so eminently fitted to develop. At the *Apollinare*, a Roman Seminary where these studies are held in honor, he has introduced a special and superior course of Greek, Latin, and Italian Philology, for those who have completed the regular curriculum of studies. There, too, he has founded chairs for the Oriental languages: Hebrew, Aramaic, Arabic, Armenian and Coptic, and to each has appointed specialists, under whose care rich results may be expected.

To promote medical and surgical science, he has bought and combined with the Vatican Library two choice collections of medical works, selected by two of Italy's most learned physicians. These books, it is needless to say, are available to the public. The united collections amount to ten thousand volumes, and embrace rare and famous works, both ancient and modern.

Nor have the fine arts been neglected. To take but a few instances: he has restored the Lateran Basilica to its former splendor, adding to it an *Apsis*, or choir, in keeping with the magnificence of the whole. The Basilica of St. Clement has gained new beauty from the new chapel of Sts. Cyrillus and Methodius. He has erected, in the Vatican garden *Della Pigna*, a column commemorative of the last Ecumenical Council; he has enriched the Borgia Museum with a rare Ethnographic collection, and the Vatican Museum with the statue of *Deus Fidius*, a Sabine work of great antiquity and perfectly preserved; he has restored and enlarged the Studio for the Mosaic works at the Vatican, and he has brought to light, and presented to the admiring study of the Artist world, the treasure of *Gobelins*, so wonderful in design, so perfect in execution.

Leo has been even more solicitous for the instruction of the people at large. He has appointed a commission of Cardinals and Roman Patricians to superintend the education of youth of both sexes in the public schools; and has generously taken upon himself the expenditures necessary for their support. The same year (1879) he caused twenty-nine additional schools to be opened, and many of those founded by Pius IX were greatly improved. Not a year has since passed without an increase in the number of schools, and despite the weight of many cares, Leo has given these schools his most earnest attention, acquainting himself constantly with their

progress, their needs, and their good results. To encourage teacher
and pupil alike, he has left nothing undone, bestowing on the one
all manner of help and sympathy, and on the other every encouraging gift that might stir up a noble spirit of emulation.

And now one last trait of the virtues of Leo, a trait all the
more remarkable, when we remember that the Holy See has been
despoiled and deprived of all regular revenues. In Rome, he has
ever been the Father of the needy. No pious work of charity has
called in vain for his encouragement, or still more substantial help.
In 1884 he paid out a million lire to erect a cholera hospital.
Through the parish priests, he has been accustomed to distribute
among the poor, not once, but several times a year, sums varying
from twelve to thirty thousand francs. His charity, however, has
by no means been confined to Rome. Among all nations, the
victims of flood, fire, earthquakes, hurricanes and famine, have
found in him a tender Father. The disasters which fell upon the
people of Ireland, Belgium, France, Austria, Greece, and even
remote China, were softened by his words of sympathy, and less-
ened by his generous help. The treasures from which he has so
freely drawn are the fruit of his children's love, *the Peter's Pence*,
contributed from all parts of the world. And while he returns
love for love, help for help, he shows them, as it were, his fatherly
heart beating in sympathy for their many sorrows.

A Protestant writer, describing Leo XIII, says: " *I should
gladly have added some darker shades to this flattering picture; but
in vain have I inquired of the most pronounced enemies of the Church
to find the least blemish.*" In fact his enemies, whether political or
religious, however much they may criticize his particular course of

action, as viewed from their standpoint, have never yet impeached his character, underrated his ability, or doubted the nobility of his intentions. The whole world recognizes in Leo XIII the

> "Man with heart, head, hand,
> Like some of the simple great ones gone."

The whole world recognizes in him great natural ability, trained by unwearied industry to that refinement and wisdom which have characterized his life. Raised to the highest dignity which merit can attain, he has applied time and talent to the welfare of all. Viewing his labors as a whole, his special mission has been to calm the storm of prejudice and hatred, so long raging, both amongst peoples and governments, against the Papacy, by three well defined methods. First, he has elevated the standard of culture among the clergy; he has, in the next place, clearly shown that true civilization and the new wonders of science, not only are not hostile to the Church's teaching, but are encouraged and developed by her endeavors; and, lastly, he has convinced the rulers of nations that the spirit of the Catholic body far from being a hindrance is the staunchest support to civil sovereignty.

In person, Leo XIII, commands respect and devotedness. Tall and of slender build, his mien is striking and majestic; and there is in his carriage a graciousness which eminently befits him. His manners are characterized by dignity, straightforwardness and benevolence. His eyes kindly in expression and undimmed by years, seem to penetrate the thoughts and feelings of those with whom he speaks. His conversation is fluent and to the point. In addition to his native tongue, he speaks, it may be added,

French, German and Latin with ease and elegance. Such is the man whose poems are here given to the public: and, considering his busy life, we may well wonder how he should have had time to compose them. Not only are they faultless in their pure Latinity, but they are distinguished for lofty and noble thought. It may be justly said that they reflect the charm and character of their illustrious author: and we have no doubt, that all who are acquainted with the life and achievements of Leo XIII, will read with sympathetic interest those effusions of his gentle, pious and noble nature.

AN. CHRIST. MDCCCLXXXI.

IN

HERCVLANVM

ET

CONSTANTIVM

EPISCOPOS MARTYRES

𝕳𝖞𝖒𝖓𝖎

LEONIS XIII P. M.

TESTES ANIMI

OBSEQVIIQVE SVI

Hymns

OF

POPE LEO XIII

In Honor

OF

HERCULANUS AND CONSTANTIUS

MARTYR-BISHOPS

1881

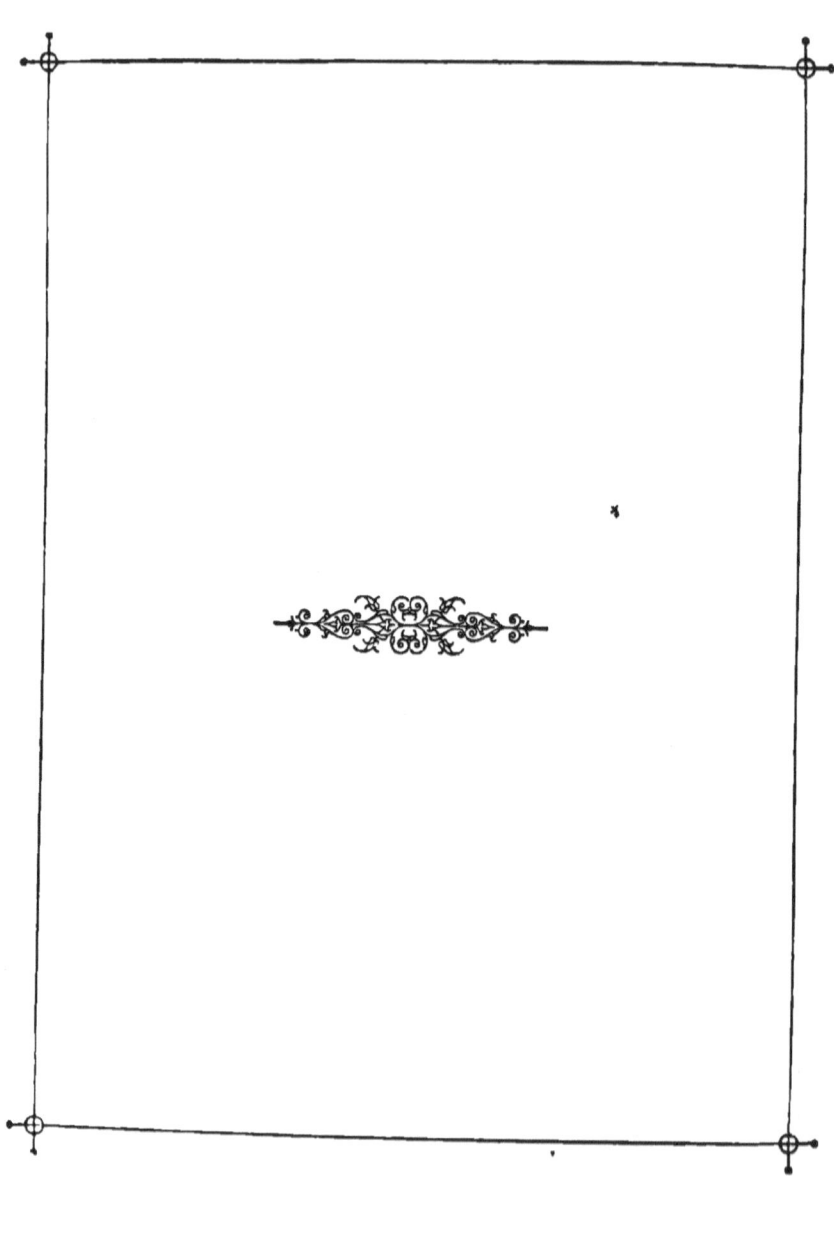

St. Herculanus.

HERCVLANVS, insigni sanctitate vir, Perusinorum Epis-
copatum ea tempestate gerebat, cum Gothorum copiae Perusiam obsiderent. Civitate capta, capite caesus est. Demortui
corpus extra muros proiectum humaniores quidam viri honesta
sepultura affecerunt. Quod quadraginta post diebus cum re-
duces in urbem cives effodissent, in aede Petri Principis Apo-
stolorum sanctiore loco composituri, integrum atque omni parte
incorruptum invenerunt, sic praeterea conglutinata ad collum
cervice, ut vestigia incisionis nulla apparerent.[1] Hunc Perusini Patronum caelestem salutarem venerantur et colunt; cuius
honori aedem a solo aedificatam maiorum pietas dedicavit.

[1] Ex Lib. III. Dial. S. Gregorii Magni.

THE saintly Herculanus was Bishop of Perugia when it was besieged by the Goths. On the capture of the city, he was beheaded and his body thrown without the walls, where it was buried by some charitable persons. Forty days later, when the citizens, on their return, disinterred his remains to place them in the church of St. Peter, Prince of the Apostles, they found the body entire and incorrupt. The head, moreover, was re-united to the trunk so that no traces of the decapitation were visible.[1] Perugia venerates St. Herculanus as its patron and heavenly protector, and has erected a church, dedicated to his name.

[1] Dial. St. Greg. B. III.

St. Herculanus.

TVTELA praesens patriae
 Salve, Herculane: filiis
 Adsis, precamur, annuo
 Qui te celèbrant cantico.

Furens Getharum ab algidis
 Devectus oris Totila,
 Turres Perusî et moenia
 Hoste obsidebat barbaro.

Iamque ingruebat arcibus
 Clades suprema: angustiis
 Urbs pressa ubique: civium
 Ubique luctus personat.

At pastor invictus vigil
 Stas, Herculane; et anxio
 Pavore fracta pectora
 Metu et soluta roboras.

St. Herculanus.

HAIL, Herculanus, champion brave,
Still prompt our fatherland to save,
Thy children bless, as in their verse
Each year thy glories they rehearse.

Down from far Gothland's icy coasts
Sweep Totila's resistless hosts,
He dooms Perugia's walls and towers,
And girds her round with ruthless powers.

Her ramparts totter to their fall
And ruin grimly broods o'er all;
The town is straitened everywhere
And dismal wailings rend the air.

But Herculanus watch doth hold;
Undaunted shepherd, o'er his fold
In trembling frames new strength instils
And faltering breasts with courage fills.

Ardens et ore: "pro fide
   Pugnate avita, filii;
   Dux ipse vester; Numini
   Servate templa, et patriam."

Hac voce genti reddita
   Insueta virtus et vigor;
   Mens una cunctis, proelio
   Certare forti et vincere.

Septem vel annos, te duce,[1]
   Urbem stetisse est proditum;
   Et barbarorum copias
   Caesas, retusos impetus.

Praecurris omnes; occidis
   Spectandus invicta fide,
   Virtute frangi nescia,
   Et glorioso funere;

Namque urbe subiecta dolo
   Non vi, occupatis moenibus,
   Dulci pro ovili sanguinem
   Vitamque laetus fundere,

With burning words: " Perugians, stand!
Fight for the faith of fatherland;
Your leader I; strike, strike for God,
Your altars and your native sod."

His voice gives nerves the strength of steel,
Gives hearts the valor heroes feel;
One purpose gleams in every eye:
" On to the fight and victory!"

For seven long years, our legends tell,[1]
The fortress walls he guarded well;
Before his shock the invaders reeled,
Their best blood oft bedewed the field.

Brave heart! outstripping e'en the brave,
You fell, but in your fall you gave
Example fair of steadfast faith,
Of dauntless soul, of glorious death.

By craft, not arms, the city falls,
The foeman's sentries pace the walls:
Your veins a city's ransom hold—
What bliss! you die to save your fold!

Desaevientis Totilae
    Iussu, sub ictum cuspidis
    Procumbis insons victima,
    Auctus corona martyrum.

Et nunc beata caelitum
    Regnans in aula, patriam
    Pastor, Patronus, et Parens
    Felix bonusque sospitas.

Laetare Etrusca civitas[2]
    Tanta refulgens gloria;
    Attolle centum gestiens
    Caput decorum turribus.

Novo impetita proelio
    Ausus repellas impios,
    Et usque fac renideas
    Fide Herculani pulcrior.

---

[1] Huius spatium obsidionis historici recentiores haud longius septem mensibus producunt. Quam sententiam nec affirmare, nec refellere in animo est.

[2] Perusia, veteri italicarum regionum descriptione, Etruriae finibus continebatur, cum Etruscorum gens Tyrrheno mari et Apenino, Macra et Tiberi fluviis terminaretur.

Forth comes fierce Totila's command :
You fall beneath the headsman's hand.
O stainless victim ! your renown
Is brightened by the martyr's crown.

And now, while in those courts you reign
Of bliss-crowned souls, our country deign,
O Pastor, Patron, Father, still
To speed to fortune, guard from ill.

Etruria's pride, fair city, clad [2]
With glory's vesture, Oh ! be glad ;
Lift high your brows, whose diadem
A hundred circling turrets gem.

When other foes their onset make,
Be brave ! their impious fury break.
Your Patron's faith still light your way,
Grow lovelier yet beneath its ray.

---

[1] Recent historians are of opinion that the siege did not last over seven months.   This is the place neither to confirm, nor gainsay their statement.

[2] According to the ancient geography of Italy, Perugia was within the limits of Etruria, when the boundaries of the latter were the Tyrrhene Sea and the Apennines, the Macra and Tiber rivers.

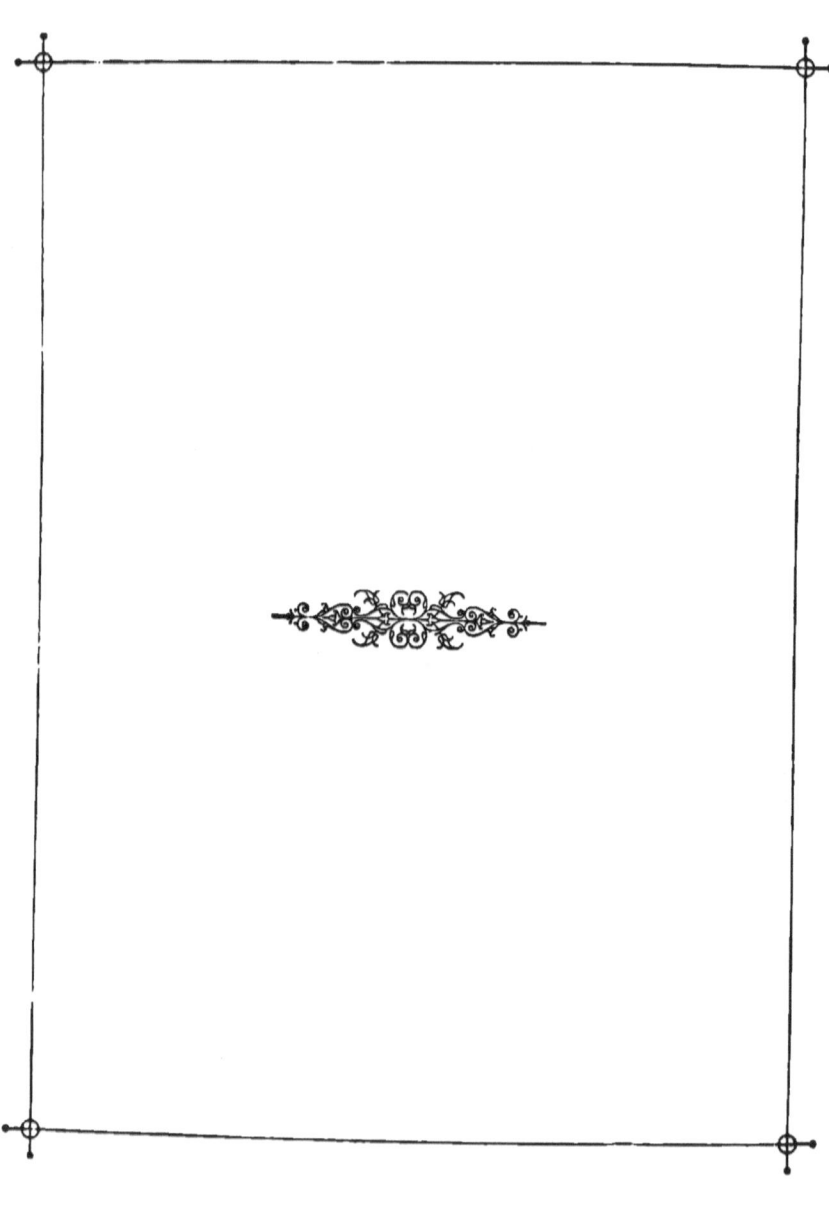

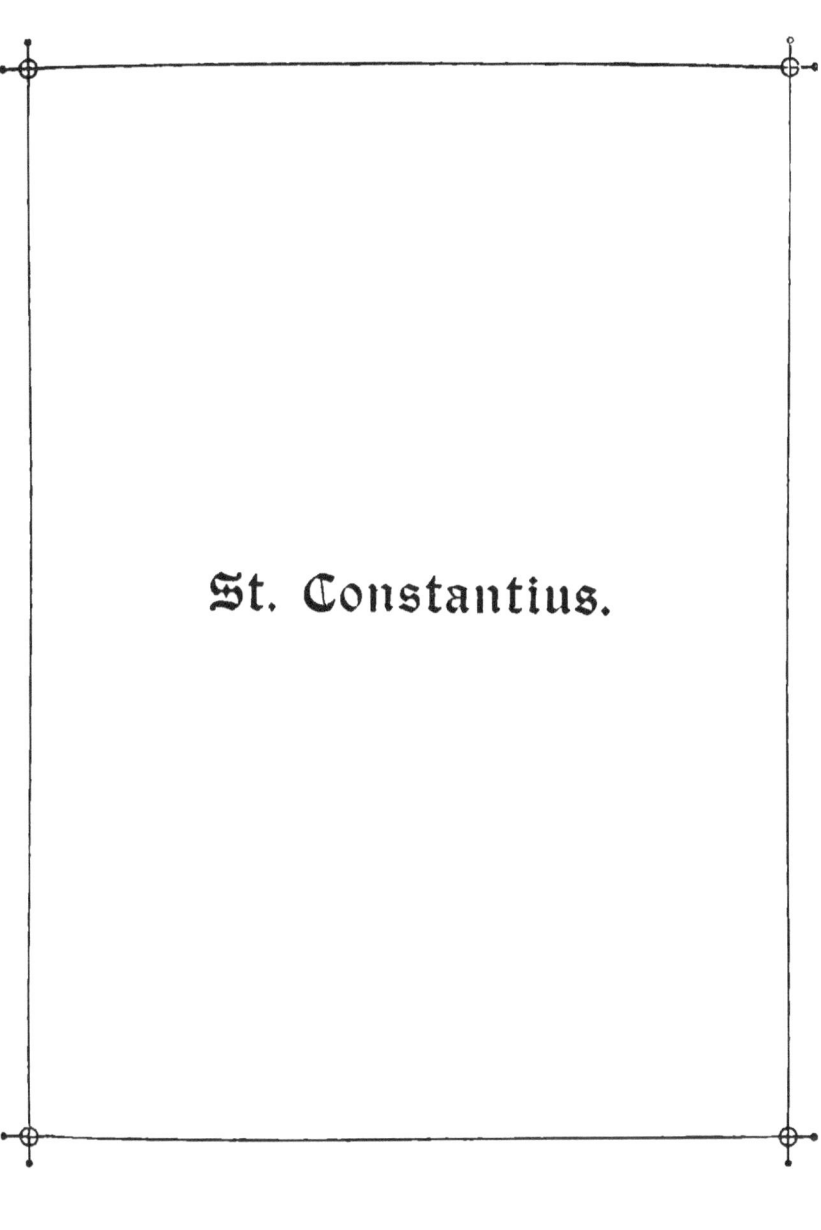

St. Constantius.

CONSTANTIVS Perusiae christianis parentibus natus, virtute aetatem antegressus, Episcopus patriae suae factus est. Is propter studium christiani nominis multa dictu gravia, perpessu aspera iuvicto animo pertulit. Nam primum pugnis contundi iussus, deinde in thermis includi septuplo vehementius accensis; sed‧ aquis Dei nutu repente tepefactis, e summo discrimine evasit incolumis. Mox prunarum cruciatu fortissime perfunctus, conjicitur in custodiam: unde christianorum opera extractum satellites imperatorii comprehendunt, et vi vulnerum prope conficiunt. Continuo tamen ille divinitus convaluit: tunc Assisium in carcerem rapitur. Paullo post illinc eductus, cum quamlibet carnificinam subire mallet, quam a proposito disseminandae catholicae religionis desistere, idcirco in trivio apud Fulginium nobile martyrium fecit, Marco Aurelio Vero Imperatore, Sotero Pontifice maximo. Sacrum eius corpus inhumatum proiectum Levianus, magna pietate vir, domo Fulginio, ab Angelo in somnis admonitus, venerabundus feretro composuit. Quod cum Perusiam deduceretur, ea res miraculo fuit, quod sacrarum reliquiarum vectores repente lumen oculorum recepere. Martyrem fortissimum Perusini summa religione colunt, eiusque memoriam, templo extructo, consecrarunt.

CONSTANTIUS was born at Perugia of Christian parents, and possessing virtue beyond his years, was made Bishop of that city. His zeal for the Christian faith was the source to him of many sufferings, painful even to hear, and bitter indeed to undergo: yet he bore them with unwavering courage. For, after he had been cruelly buffeted by his persecutors, he was shut up in the hot baths raised to sevenfold their usual heat: from which it pleased God that he should issue unharmed, the waters having only a pleasing warmth to his body. He then valiantly endured the torture of burning coals, and after this was cast into prison. Rescued by Christians, the minions of the Emperor seized him again and wounded him so that he nearly died.

Through the divine help he soon regained his strength: when he was thrown into prison at Assisi. A little while and he was brought forth, and willing to suffer every cruelty rather than give up his purpose of teaching the Catholic verity, he underwent a glorious martyrdom at the cross-roads in Foligno, under the Emperor Marcus Aurelius Verus and the Pontiff Soter. His body was cast forth unburied. Levian, a pious man of Foligno, reverently placed it on a bier, being advised thereto by an angel. While it was being borne to Perugia, the blind men who were carrying the sacred remains, suddenly received their sight. The Perugians cherish the greatest devotion for the valiant martyr and have a church to his memory.

St. Constantius.

I.

FAVETE linguis; hinc procul
    Este, O profani; crastinus [1]
    Sollemniis Constantii
    Sacer dies est martyris.

O Dive, praesens O tuae
    Salus decusque patriae!
    Redi auspicatus, iam redi
    Umbris colendus gentibus.

Te heroa, te fortissimum
    Efferre caelo Martyrem
    Oblita laudes Caesarum
    Turrena gestit canticis.

Hyems rigescit, [2] asperis
    Montes pruinis albicant,
    Solisque crines frigido
    Irrorat imbre Aquarius.

St Constantius.

I.

SILENCE awhile, ye babblers light:
Ye hardened worldly hearts, away!
The morrow's solemn sacred rite
Shall sanctify the Martyr's day.[1]

Thy country's boast and bulwark thou,
O godlike man, propitious hear
While Umbrian folk breathe forth their vow,
And to their prayers lend gracious ear!

Unheeding what the Caesar claims
The tower-girt town in joyous lays
Thy name, O martyred hero, frames,
Filling the welkin with thy praise.

Winter's hard clutch has blanched the height
And stiffened all the glad champaign:
The pathway of the sun's kind light
Is blurred with floods of chilling rain.[2]

At bruma non desaeviens,
    Non atra caeli nubila
    Cives morantur annuis
    Rite exsilire gaudiis.

Nox en propinquat: cerneres
    Fervere turbis compita,
    Late per umbram cerneres
    Ardere colles ignibus;[3]

Urbisque ferri ad moenia
    Incessu et ore supplici
    Senes, viros, cum matribus
    Longo puellas agmine.

Ut ventum, ubi ara Martyris
    Corusca lychnis emicat,
    Festiva turba civium
    Irrumpit ardens, clamitat:

"O Pastor, e caelo O Parens
    Constanti, adesto filiis:"
    Pressis sepulcro et dulcia
    Figit labellis oscula.

But all the elemental strife,
And sky with clouds of pregnant black,
Stays not the civic joy so rife,
Nor holds the yearly pageant back.

Night falls upon the town: see how
The ways are seething with the throng!
And look! there on the hill's veiled brow
A thousand bonfires leap along;[3]

Then to the city walls advance
With stately tread and suppliant eyes,
Long lines of maids, with bated glance,
Matrons, strong sires, and elders wise.

And when they reach the Martyr's shrine,
Where brightly blazing tapers flare,
The joyous throng in serried line
Beseech the Martyr's potent care:

"Constantius, guardian, heavenly sire,
Thy little ones Oh! deign to bless!"
And kindling with their love's chaste fire
Warm kisses on his tomb they press.

Iesu, tibi sit gloria,
    Qui das triumphum Martyri,
    Cum Patre et almo Spiritu
    In saeculorum saecula.

II.

PANDITVR templum; facibus renidet
Ara Constanti: celebrate nomen
Dulce Pastoris, memoresque fastos
    Dicite cantu.

Impios ritus et inane fulmen
Risit indignans Iovis et Quirini;
Obtulit ferro iuveniie pectus,
    Obtulit igni.

Jesu, the Martyr's strength, to Thee,
The Father, and the Paraclete,
Be glory for eternity,
O Triune God, all Infinite.

II.

LO ! the temple is open : Constantius' shrine
Glows bright within from the torches' flame :
Come, singers, with filial voices twine
  A wreath of song to your Patron's name :
    Blend choric lays with prayers.

All their impious rites and Jove's bolts inane,
  And the various gods whom the Pagans name
He laughs to scorn : and, unrecking the pain,
  To the sword's keen point and the biting flame
    His youthful breast he bares.

Aestuant thermae saliente flamma:
   Densa plebs circum stat anhela: Praetor
   Clamat: "I, lictor, calida rebellem
      Merge sub unda."

Mergitur: plantas simul unda tinxit,
   Frigidus ceu fons per amoena florum
   Defluens, blando recreata mulcet
      Membra lavacro.

Vulgus immoto stupet ore; Praetor
   Frendet elusus; scelerum ministris
   Mandat, obstrictum manicis recondant
      Carceris antro.

Vincla nil terrent; Fidei Magister
   Liber effaris, Vigilum docendo
   Pectora emollis: stygiusque fugit
      Mentibus error.

The baths, made hot with a roaring fire,
    Seethe fiercely and fast, and the breathless crowd
Still closer press as the flames mount higher:
    "Plunge the stubborn knave," shrieks the Praetor loud,
        "In yonder bubbling wave!"

They plunge him in: but as fainting flowers
    A cool font freshens with grateful dews,
So the boiling bath his body dowers
    With a strength that quivers through all his thews,
        And balmy coolness gave.

Thereupon dumb fear smote the gaping throng:
    But the Praetor, foiled, in a frenzy cries
To his caitiff slaves: "With manacles strong
    Let the man be bound most cautious wise,
        And thrust in dungeon deep!"

Chains quell him not: but with fearless voice
    He rings Faith's truth in his gaolers' ears:
They listen, they yield, and their hearts rejoice
    That the cloud is scattered that held them for years
        In error's numbing sleep.

Saevior contra rabies tyranni
  Flagrat; insontem lacerat flagellis,
  Sauciat ferro, rigidaque plantas
        Compede torquet.

Nec datum immani sat adhuc furori;
  Hostiam diris agit, et Deorum
  Numini spreto vovet immolandam
        Caede cruenta.

Corpus in limo iacet interemptum:
  At pius forti celebrandus ausu
  Luce pallenti vigilans ad umbram
        Carceris, ima

Septa pervadit Levianus; artus
  Colligit sparsos; caput ense truncum
  Rite componens fovet, et beata
        Condit in urna.

More passionate still swells the tyrant's breast:
   The pure young flesh feels the branding rod,
And the sword's keen gash : while the feet that pressed
   So firm on the way to the Throne of God
      Hard massy fetters cut.

But his wrath not yet does the tyrant bate :
   To his gods contemned and their vengeful ire
He dooms the youth till his bloody fate,
   Cut, and racked, and torn, with torture dire,
      The Furies' hate may glut.

Lo! at last, done to death, cold and stark he lies :
   Even earth's warm clod may not cover his bones ;
But when twilight's grey is drawn o'er the skies,
   Levian watchful comes where the wall's grim stones
      Frown down like sentries stern.

Be his noble deed through the wide world spread !
   Each torn bruised limb, with such reverent grace
Does he gather up, and the sword-gashed head :
   Then his hands, all gently, the relics place
      In seemly funeral urn.

Grande portentum! sacra membra in urbem
Quattuor latis humeris reportant
Lucis expertes, subitoque visus
     Munere gaudent.

Redditur Pastor patriae, refulgens
Aureis vittis et honore palmae,
Septus aeterna superum corona
     Redditur heros.

Dive, quem templis veneramur Umbris,
Umbriae fines placido revisens
Lumine, exoptata reduc opimae
     Gaudia pacis.

Dive, Pastorem tua in urbe quondam
Infula cinctum, socium et laborum,
Quem pius tutum per iter superna
     Luce regebas,

But a miracle rare!—on their shoulders broad
   While the sacred burden four blind men bear
To Perugia town, by the gift of the Lord
   Their sightless balls with an awe-thrilled stare
      In vision grasp the world.

With martyr's palm and fillets of gold
   To his fatherland is the Shepherd given,
While circle around him in numbers untold
   Heaven's deathless true, who have also striven
      Where Hell its legions hurled.

O Saint, whom we cherish in Umbria's fanes,
   On our Umbrian homes bend thy gaze benign!
Lead back to us Peace, with its laden wains,
   That our hearts be at rest, and no longer pine
      For joys too long delayed!

O Saint, he who erst in this city bore
   Thy bishop's mitre, thy bishop's care,
Who full oft did as client thy aid implore
   That with tread as unswerving as thine he might fare
      In paths thy footsteps made;

Nunc Petri cymbam tumidum per aequor
　　Ducere, et pugnae per acuta cernis
　　Spe bona certaque levare in altos
　　　　Lumina montes.

Possit O tandem, domitis procellis,
　　Viscre optatas LEO victor oras;
　　Occupet tandem vaga cymba portum
　　　　Sospite cursu.

---

[1] Scriptus est hymnus ob praeludium diei festi.

[2] Sacra sollemnia ob memoriam S. Constantii aguntur IV Kal. Febr.

[3] Mos antiquissimus Perusiae fuit, ut quotannis pridie natalis S. Constantii sollemnis pompa ad pomerium vesperi duceretur, viris comitantibus ac dona ferentibus; quae "supplicatio luminum" idcirco appellata est, quod urbs tota facibus cereisque, suburbium ignibus ad laetitiam per noctem collucoret. Pulcra extant de ea supplicatione legum municipalium decreta.

Now, as Peter's bark through the rising sea
He guides, and in war waged 'gainst the wrong,
Lifts his eyes to the hills of eternity,
    With a hope that is sure and a hope that is strong,
        God's help to his oppressed.

May he, LEO, behold, when the storms are laid,
As a victor, at length the longed-for shore ;
And the wandering bark, safe anchorage made,
    May it, too, be brought through the tempest's roar
        To God-calmed port of rest.

---

[1] This hymn was written for the Saint's feast.

[2] The Solemnity in memory of St. Constantius occurs on the 29th of January.

[3] It is a very old custom at Perugia to have a grand procession every year out-side the walls, on the evening of the Vigil of the Feast of Saint Constantius, when the men march and bear offerings. This function is known as the "Festival of Lights" (*La Festa dei Lumi*), as the whole town is lit with torches and tapers and joyous bonfires blaze through all the suburbs the night through. Many beautiful decrees in regard to this festival have been passed by the city.

Ad Vincentivm Pavanivm e S. I.

AN. MDCCCXXII.

Nomine, Vincenti, quo tu, Pavane, vocaris
Parvulus atque infans Peccius ipse vocor.[1]

Quas es virtutes magnas, Pavane, sequutus
O utinam possem Peccius ipse sequi.

---

[1] Auctori ad sacrum baptisma imposita fuerant nomina Ioachimo, Vincentio, Raphaeli, Aloisio. Sed mater eius Vincentium appellari maluit ob honorem Vincentii Ferrerii, cuius extitit cultrix eximia. Quod ille nomen serius cum Ioachimo commutavit.

To Vincent Pavani, S. J.

1822.

IN childhood's hour I joyed to claim
As mine, O Vincent, thy dear name;[1]
Ah! could I claim not name alone,
But virtue great as thou hast shown!

---

[1] In baptism, the author received the names of Joachim, Vincent, Raphael and Aloysius. His mother, through her devotion to St. Vincent Ferrer, called him Vincent; but his own choice in later years was Joachim.

De Invaletvdine Sva.

AN. MDCCCXXX.

Pvber bis denos, Ioachim, vix crescis in annos;
  Morborum heu quanta vi miser obrueris!

Iuverit hos fando tristes memorare dolores,
  Et vitae aerumnas dicere carminibus.

Nocte vigil, tarda componis membra quiete,
  Viribus effoetis esca nec ulla tuum

Cruda levat stomachum; depresso lumine ocelli
  Caligant; ictum saepe dolore caput.

Mox gelida arentes misere depascitur artus
  Febris edax, mox et torrida discruciat.

Iam macies vultu apparet, iam pectus anhelum est;
  Deficis en toto corpore languidulus.

On his Ill Health.

1830.

O HAPLESS Joachim! diseases' prey,
Ere twice ten summers doomed to slow decay!

Thy cruel griefs in rhymes shall I relate,
And mourn, alas! thy too unhappy fate.

Dull, dreary nights and tardy slumbers thine;
Sleep flees the couch on which thy limbs recline.

Kind nurture seems not potent to restore
Thy strength; thy sunken eye is clouded o'er;

And throbs thy weary head; thy frame by turns
Lies chilled by fever's stroke, now fiercely burns.

Wan are thy cheeks, and weak thy panting breast
By crushing aches each languid limb oppressed.

Quid tibi blandiris, longos quid prospicis annos?
    Atropos horrendum mortis adurget iter.

Tunc ego: "non trepida frangar formidine: mortem,
    Dum properat, fortis laetus et opperiar.

Non me labentis pertentant gaudia vitae,
    Aeternis inhians nil peritura moror.

Attingens patriam, felix erit advena, felix
    Si valet ad portum ducere nauta ratem."

Why cling to life, why vainly shun thy doom,
While wasting illness urges to the tomb?

Then I : shrink not my heart though dread my fate,
Death's hastening footsteps joyful I await.

No fleeting pleasures can my soul allure,
A land I seek whose joys shall e'er endure.

Gladly the wanderer hails his native land,
Gladly the sailor sees the port at hand.

Rogerivs A. C. Adolescens.[1]

EFFRONTEM MVLIEREM DEPELLIT.

QVID fucata genas, quid vultu habituque proterva
   Mente agitas? Procul hinc siste, Amarylli, pedem.

Letiferum stillas meretricio ob ore venenum,
   Et corde infandum, proh pudor, ulcus alis.

---

[1] Auctori amicus et in studiis litterarum socius.

The Repulse of Vice.[1]

FACE aglow with tricking art,
Eyes that wanton glances dart,
    'Vot'ress of the Cyprian Queen,
    Fair without and foul within,
On what ruin dost thou start?
    Well is thy treason known!
On thy lips, pernicious breath,
In thy heart is horrid death;
    Temptress unmasked, begone!

---

[1] Roger A. C., a friend and fellow-student of the author's, repels the advances of a profligate woman.

Fons Loqvitvr.[1]

LENITER exiliens Pandulphi e colle superno,
  Huc e nativis deferor unda iugis.

Nam qui romani IOACHIMUS PECCIUS ostri
  Primus natale hoc auxit honore solum,

Per caecos terrae, plumbo ducente, meatus
  Oblitam patriae me iubet ire viam.

Improvisa quidem, sed gratior advena vobis
  Ultro, municipes, candida, inempta fluo.

The Fountain.[1]

FROM Pandolfo's lofty crest,
    Erst my sunny mountain home,
Noiseless, knowing not to rest,
    Joyous to the vale I come.

Princely PECCI bade me come;
    He who first in purple clad,
Honor-crowned of sacred Rome,
    Made his native valley glad.

Dark my way beneath the fell,
    Half my life in lead compressed;
Still I bid my home farewell,
    Come I must at his behest.

All unlooked-for, too, nor less
    Welcome for the gifts I bear—
Beauty, cleanness, healthfulness,
    Household blessings sweet and fair.

Huc ergo properate: adsum nam sacra saluti,
Munditiae, vitaeque usibus et γάρισιν.

¹ Aquam saluberrimi haustus Carpinetum adducendam curavit an. MDCCCLXIV.

Hither! of my crystal treasure
Glad and grateful share the store,
Flowing for your use and pleasure,
Free and stintless evermore.

[1] In 1864, the author had a stream of clear, wholesome water from the mountains, introduced into his native town, Carpineto.

De Se Ipso.

AN. MDCCCLXXV.

QVAM flore in primo felix, quam laeta Lepinis.
  Orta jugis, patrio sub lare, vita fuit![1]

Altrix te puerum Vetulonia suscipit ulnis,
  Atque in Loyolaea excolit aede pium.[2]

Mutia dein Romae tenuere palatia; doctis
  Florentem studiis Academia tenet;[3]

Tempore quo, meminisse juvat, praedivite vena
  MANERA et Patrum nobilis illa cohors

Mentem alit, et puro latices de fonte recludens,
  Te Sophiae atque Dei scita verenda docet.[4]

On Himself.

A. D. 1875.

HOW happy was thy life's young dawn!
  Those days among the Lepine hills,[1]
Sweetened by all a home's dear charms,
  Serene and void of ills.

On thy first flight from that green vale
  Viterbo clasped thee, grown a boy,
And gave thee to the fostering care
  Loyola's sons employ.[2]

Rome, and the Muti's palace next:
  There, thou didst haunt that solemn hall,
Where science trains earth's noble ones,
  Made nobler by God's call,[3]

What time Mauera's brilliant mind,
  And brains with richest knowledge fraught,
In draught of learning, crystal pure,
  God's truth, and wisdom taught.[4]

Romae sacra litas; Romae tibi Iuris alumno
  Parta labore comas laurea condecorat.

Addit mox animos et vires SALA secundas,
  Princeps romano murice conspicuus;

Auspice quo cursum moliris, mente volutans
  Usque tua tanti dicta diserta senis.[5]

Dulcis Parthenope, Beneventum dein tenet, aequa
  Ut lege Hirpinos imperioque regas.

Te gremio laeta excipiens Turrena salutat,
  Rectorem atque ducem vividus Umber habet.[6]

Sed maiora manent: en chrismatis auctus honore
  Pontificis nutu Belgica regna petis,

Atque tenes, adserturus sanctissima Petri,
  Romanae et fidei credita iura tibi.[7]

Rome saw thee with Christ's priesthood crowned:
    Then round thy brow she also saw,
Reward to hardy toil decreed,
    The laurels of the Law.

What counsel wise, what generous aid
    A prince in Rome's bright purple lent
To shape thy manhood's young emprise!—
    Sala, the good and eloquent[5] —

Sweet Naples then, and Benevent
    Are subject to thy goodly rule:
In " Tower-town " glad, thy heart and brain
    The soulful Umbrian school.[6]

But graver, nobler duties yet
    The Pontiff's will assigns,
When on thy brow the chrism left
    Its consecrating lines.

Entrusted to thy watchful care,
    Rome's holy Faith and Peter's Right,
As Nuncio to the Belgian Court,
    Thy guardian zeal excite.[7]

Redditus at patriae. brumali e littore jussus
Ausoniae laetas et remeare plagas;

Umbros en iterum[8] fines, urbemque revisis,
Quam tibi divino flamine sponsat amor.

Iure sacro imperitas ter denos amplius annos;
Et pleno saturas ubere Pastor oves.[9]

Romano incedis Princeps spectandus in ostro,[10]
Belgarumque equitum torquis honore nites.[11]

Te pia turba, Deo pubes devota, Sacerdos
Obsequiis certant demeruisse suis.

Verum quid fluxos memoras, quid prodis honores?
Una hominem virtus ditat et una beat.

Back to thy own dear land recalled,
  Back from that chilly Northern air,
Thy sweet sunlit Italian plains
  A double radiance wear.

Lo! Umbria's border, where once more
  Hearts greet thee in the "tower-girt" town[8]
Which strongest bonds of hallowing love,
  Knit closely to thine own.

Thou bearest there for thrice ten years
  The burdens of a Shepherd true:[9]
At whose kind hands thy grateful flock
  A bounteous plenty knew.

Then prince of Holy Roman Church,
  Robed with the purple's ruddy fold,[10]
Wearing what Belgium's Knighthood prize,
  The collar of bright gold.[11]

But why recall what passeth quick?
  Why honors with thy words confess?
Virtue alone enriches man,
  Virtue alone can bless.

Scilicet hanc unam, aevo iam iabente, sequaris,
   Ad Superos tutum quae tibi pandat iter.

Aeterna donec compostus pace quiescas,
   Sidereae ingressus regna beata domus.

Ah! miserans adsit Deus eventusque secundet:
   Aspiret votis Virgo benigna tuis.[1]

---

[1] Ortus Carpineti die 2 Martii a. 1810 ex coniugibus Ludovico Peccio et Anna Prosperia, ad octavum aetatis annum in domo paterna moratur. *Carpinetum* est oppidum in Volscis prope Signiam in sinu montium quos *Lepinos* vocant.

[2] A. 1818 cum Josepho fratre Viterbium mittitur, et Sodalibus e Societate Iesu instituendus traditur.

This make thine own, and this alone:
Then, when earth's hours their course complete,
A path secure to heaven's fair courts
Shall open to thy feet.

Thus in that slumber sunk at length,
Whose waking is eternity,
Their home beyond the starry skies
The saints will share with thee.

Ah! may thy God in pity deign
To give thy days that happy end:
May Christ's dear Mother, Virgin mild,
Thy toil and aims befriend.

---

[1] The author was born on the 2nd of March, 1810, at Carpineto. His parents were Louis Pecci and Anna Prosperi, with whom the little Gioacchino lived until the eighth year of his age. Carpineto, a town of the ancient Volsci, near Signia in Central Italy, is situated in a valley of the mountains known as the Lepine.

[2] In 1818, he and his brother Joseph were sent to Viterbo to receive their education at the hands of the Jesuit Fathers in that city.

[3] Defuncta matre a. 1824, apud avunculum Romae diversatur in palatio Marchionum Muti, ac deinde in Academia Nobilium Ecclesiasticorum.

[4] P. Franciscus Manera S. I., vir ingenio et doctrina praestantissimus, aliique Patres clarissimi, quos in Lyceo Gregoriano Philosophiae et Theologiae magistros habuit, Andreas Carafa, I. B. Pianciani, Antonius Ferrarini, Ioannes Perrone, Ioseph Rizzi, Joannes Curi, Antonius Kohlmann, etc.

[5] Ioseph Antonius Sala Cardinalis peculiari benevolentia adolescentem complectitur, et sapientibus monitis et consiliis plurimum juvat.

[6] Laurea doctorali insignitus, post susceptum sacerdotium, a Gregorio XVI. P. M. inter antistites urbanos domus Pontificalis adsciscitur a. 1837, ac postea provinciarum Beneventanae et Perusinae gubernator constituitur.

[7] In sacro Consistorio, habito die 27 Januarii a. 1843, Archiepiscopus Damiatensis eligitur, et Apostolicae Sedis Nuntius ad Belgas mittitur.

[8] Perusia a turribus, quibus muniebatur, dicta est Turrena.

[9] A. 1846 a Gregorio XVI. P. M., in sacro Consistorio die 19 Januarii habito, ad Sedem Perusinam provehitur.

[10] A. 1853, in sacro Consistorio habito die 19 Decembris, a Pio IX. P. M., S. R. E. Presbyter Cardinalis renuntiatur titulo S. Chrysogoni.

[11] Belgica Legatione perfunctus, a Leopoldo I. Belgarum Rege inter equites torquatos Ordinis Leopoldiani adlectus est.

³ Upon the death of his mother, in 1824, he went to Rome, and at first lived with his uncle in the palace of the Marquesses Muti, but afterwards resided at the Academy of Noble Ecclesiastics.

⁴ Father Francis Manera, S. J., was a man of great ability and learning. The other eminent Fathers whom he had as Professors of Philosophy and Theology in the Gregorian College, were Andrew Carafa, J. B. Pianciani, Antony Ferrarini, John Perrone, Joseph Rizzi, John Curi, Antony Kohlmann, etc.

⁵ Cardinal Joseph Antony Sala favored the youth in many ways, and afforded him great assistance by his wise counsels and admonitions.

⁶ After ordination to the priesthood, he was raised to the degree of Doctor of Laws, was placed among the domestic Prelates of the Pontifical Palace by Pope Gregory XVI, in 1837, and afterwards appointed Governor of the Provinces of Benevento and Perugia.

⁷ In the sacred Consistory, held January 27th, 1843, he was preconised Archbishop of Damietta, and sent to Belgium as Papal Nuncio.

⁸ Perugia is called Turrena, the tower-girt, from the many towers that formed part of the city's defences.

⁹ In the Consistory of January 19, 1846, he was translated to the See of Perugia by Gregory XVI.

¹⁰ In 1853, in the sacred Consistory, held on the 19th of December, he was proclaimed by Pope Pius IX, Cardinal priest with the title of St. Chrysogonus.

¹¹ At the end of his mission to Belgium, he was honored, by King Leopold I, with the collar of a Knight of the Order of Leopold.

GERTRVDI · STERBINIAE

VIRGINI · SALESIANAE

INNOCENTISSIMAE

QVAE

VTI · CHRISTO · IESV · PLACERET

ASPERA · MVLTA · FORTITER · TVLIT

EADEM

RIGIDIORVM · ALVMNA · ET · CVLTRIX · VIRTVTVM

MVNERIBVS · LABORIBVS · QVE · SANCTE · PERFVNCTA

MATVRA · CAELO

LAETA · LIBENS

IN · PACE · CHRISTI · CONQVIEVIT

III · NON. · FEBR. · AN. · MDCCCLXXIII

ANNOS · NATA · XLIII · M · I · D · XXVI

IVLIVS · FRATER

SORORI · INCOMPARABILI

SE · SVOS · QVE · COMMENDAT

IN MEMORY OF

GERTRUDE STERBINI,

NUN OF THE VISITATION ORDER,

WHO IN HER PURE AND SAINTLY LIFE,

FOR HER DEAR SAVIOUR'S LOVE

BORE MANY A HARDSHIP BRAVELY:

UNTIL PERFECT IN ALL HOLINESS,

HER DUTY FAITHFULLY DONE,

RIPE FOR PARADISE,

SHE ENTERED INTO THE PEACE OF CHRIST,

WITH GLAD REJOICING,

ON THE 3RD OF FEBRUARY, 1873,

AGED 43 YEARS, 1 MONTH, 26 DAYS;

TO HER, HIS SISTER BEYOND COMPARE,

HER BROTHER JULIUS

COMMENDS HIMSELF AND HIS.

GERTRVDES, O sacra Deo castissima virgo,
Grata, precor, IVLI vota dolentis habe.

Fortunata soror, Superum quae vesceris aura,
Nostri sollicitam te vetus urat amor.

E caelo memor usque tuis succurrere discas,
Iufensisque leves anxia corda malis.

Atque olim Ersiliam, natos, dulcesque parentes,
Meque tibi in patria iungat adauctus amor.

DEAR Gertrude, bride devoted of the Lamb,
If still there be of earthly love a care
In thine own heights of Heaven's blessed calm,
Sister, give ear to mourning Julius' prayer.

Mindful of thine, with aid in dark hours come,
With hope to anxious hearts; until with thee
My babe, Ersilia, our sweet parents, home
And I, in larger love, shall reunited be.

Sororis Opem Implorat.

SVB ALLEGORIA NAVIS.

HEV mare sollicitum spumantibus aestuat undis:
Nox heu nimbosum contegit atra polum.

Quassatur ventis, pelago iactatur in alto,
Et iam fracta ratis gurgitis ima petit.

Horremus trepidi, quatit aeger anhelitus artus:
Mors instat, iam iam nos vorat unda maris.

To the Same.[1]

SEETHING is the deep and crested
  With the foam of angry waves,
As the night steals o'er the heavens
  From its silent, sunless caves.

Shattered by the storm and drifting,
  Drifting on the maddened tide,
Onward drives the bark dismantled
  To the whirlpool deep and wide;

Onward, as we wait and tremble
  Breathless with a nameless fear,
Death before us looming grimly
  From the yawning sea-gulf near.

---

[1] Julius Sterbini implores the heavenly influence of his sister Gertrude. He represents his own needs and her kindly intervention by the allegory of a tempest-beaten ship that is rescued.

Flet genitor, resoluta comas loca questubus implet
  Coniux; cum natis anxius ipse gemens.

"O soror, inclamo, portu iam tuta beato,
  Eia adsis, nostras et miserata vices,

Fluctibus in mediis affulge sidus amicum,
  Per vada, per syrtes, O bona, tende manus:

Ocius affer opem, pontique e gurgite raptos
  Iusere sidereis ipsa benigna plagis;

Detur ubi amplexus iterare, et iungere dextras,
  Aeternum detur solvere vota Deo."

Pallid wife with locks dishevelled
Rends the air with plaintive cries;
Wail of child and moan of father
O'er the din of ocean rise.

"Sister! safe within the haven
Of the voiceless, viewless shore,
Be our Angel and befriend us
In affliction dark and sore;

Beam upon us like some lode-star
Lighting up the trackless plain,
Leading clear of shoals and quicksands
Through the dark, mysterious main;

Haste thy coming! and our frail bark,
Caught from ruin on the deep,
Homeward guide, where luminous star-worlds
Their supernal vigils keep;

Where our arms again may fold thee,
And our hands may clasp thine own,
Hymning songs of praise eternal
Round the Godhead's great white throne."

Cum esset Perusinorum Episcopus, excellentes aliquo genere sacerdotes carminibus laudare, item ex sacris virginibus optimas quasque celebrare consueverat. Carminum quoddam veluti specimen hoc loco proponitur.

I⊤ was an amiable practice of the author's, when Bishop of Perugia, to commend in verse some of his priests who distinguished themselves by peculiar merit, and also some of the religieuses of his diocese who were of eminent virtue and ability. Several pieces are here presented as specimens of his poetry in this vein.

In Nicolavm Pompilivm.[1]

PASTOR ad exemplum, Pruneti in dulcibus arvis,
    Suffecit tenero pascua laeta gregi.

Rector ad exemplum, fingenda pube peritus
    Florere hanc studiis, hanc iter atterere,

Se duce, virtutis docuit: laus inde superstes,
    Famaque Pompilium non peritura manet.

---

[1] Nicolaus Pompilius recti tenax, ad consilia prudens, curionis munere apud Prunctenses diu integreque gesto, Canonicus templi maximi Perusini factus est, sacroque Seminario regundo praefectus.

To Nicholas Pompilius.[1]

A MODEL shepherd on Prugneto's slopes
  Thy tender flock to pleasant pasture leading:
A model guide, to shape youth's plastic hopes
  To ends most high through love's ingenious pleading;
Teaching the mind to bud with wisdom's flower,
  Training the heart to be sweet virtue's shrine:
This praise is thine, not fleeting with the hour,
  But through all time, Pompilius, this is thine.

---

[1] Nicholas Pompilius, a man of solid virtues and great prudence, after filling
for a long time the post of parish-priest at Prugneto most exemplarily, was made
a Canon in the Cathedral of Perugia, and appointed Superior of the Seminary.

In Petrvm Penna.[1]

FORTVNATE senex, dulcis dum vita maneret.
Te candore animi, te pietate, fide

Acquabat nemo; laetis in rebus, in arctis
Delicium populi tu, bone pastor, eras.

---

[1] Petrus Penna curio sanctissimi exempli, mira animi simplicitate, multorum-
que recte factorum memoria clarus.

To Peter Penna.[1]

O RARE old man! through all thy life's sweet way,
A whiter soul than thine, more true, more kind
No man of us hath known: thy flock's dear stay
In weal or woe, shepherd of equal mind.

---

[1] Peter Penna was a parish-priest of the most exemplary type, widely known for his wonderful simplicity and many deeds of signal worth.

In Seraphinvm Paradisivm.[1]

QVAE subiecta oculis, vera est pastoris imago
Divae Helenes dulci pabulo alentis oves.

Quae patria et nomen fuerit si forte requiras,
Verius hoc referet picta tabella tibi.

Nam patriam dicet Paradisi in sede beatam,
Adscriptumque choris nomen in angelicis.

---

[1] Seraphinus Paradisi, parochus in castro S. Helenes integer vitae et carus ubique modestia sua.

To Serafino Paradisi.[1]

BEHOLD a faithful portrait of St. Helen's priest
Who reapeth lush green grasses that his lambs may feast.

Should'st haply ask, what name he hath, where dwelleth he,
This painted tablet shall more truly tell it thee.

It saith: his fatherland is Paradise, his name
The glowing Seraphim as theirs proclaim.

---

[1] Serafino Paradisi, pastor at Castello di S. Elena, was a man of irreproachable life, and everywhere beloved for his modesty.

In Sanctem Petrazzinivm.[1]

RELLIGIO et Pietas titulum inscripsere sepulchro
Effusae in lacrimas hunc, Petracine, tuo:

"Curio bis denis pius et mitissimus annis
Parvum sollicito pavit amore gregem.

In plebem miserans hic prodigus aeris egenam
Mirum! vel censu paupere fudit opes."

---

[1] Sanctos Petrazzinius, parochus Ecclesiae Ramaticnsis, pius in Deum, benignus in egenos, amorem omnium virtute promeruit.

To Sante Petrazzini.[1]

IN sorrow, Sante, faith and love
Have writ these words thy grave above:—

"This Shepherd loved his sheep, and fed
His flock with eucharistic bread.

And aye the needy of his fold
Were heard—though poor he lavished gold."

---

[1] Sante Petrazzini, parish-priest of Ramazzano, by his piety, his kindness to the poor and every other virtue, won for himself universal love and esteem.

In Hermelindam Montespercili

ANTISTITAM SACRARVM VIRGINVM CISTERCIENSIVM. [1]

PROGENIE illustris, verae et virtutis alumna
Virgo, Hermelinda et nomine, sacra Deo;

Coenobii custos vigil et fidissima, mater
Provida consilio, propositique tenax.

---

[1] Magistra virginum Cisterciensium ad Sanctae Iulianae per annos XXV, caritatis prudentiaeque laude insignis. Obiit die III. Iulii a. MCCCLXXII.

To Hermelind Montesperelli

ABBESS OF ST. JULIANA.[1]

UNFADING flower of noble race,
Ennobling name with virtues' grace,
The Lord's own handmaid, Hermelind:

The cloister felt thy guardian hand,
Thy mother's heart that wisely planned
With holy aim, with steadfast mind.

---

[1] She was Superioress of the Cistercian Nuns of St. Juliana for twenty-five years, and was distinguished for her charity and prudence. Her happy death occurred on the 3d of July, 1872.

In Rosalindam Bastiani

ANTISTITAM COENOBII AD S. CATHARINAE.[1]

VIRTVTES celebrare tuas, praeclaraque gesta
Quis valeat, vel quod par erit ellogium?

Ellogium *matris*: sacra inter septa senescis
Spectanda exemplis et pietate gravis.

Acclamant *matrem* concordi voce sorores,
Tu dux, tuque illis provida *mater* eras.

Ereptam terris te *matrem* nunc quoque dicunt:
Matrem cum lacrimis in sua vota vocant.

---

[1] Magisterium coenobii tres et triginta annos continuos gessit. Ob singularem animi bonitatem sacrae virgines eam familiariter appellare consueverant—*La nostra buona mamma*—Obiit die XXVI. Decembris an. MDCCCLXXI.

To Rosalind Bastiani,

ABBESS OF ST. CATHARINE.[1]

WHO might essay in fitting lays
　To tell thy virtues and fair deeds?
　Even a daughter's voice must needs
Fail somewhat in her mother's praise.

Then through long years, exemplar bright
　With grave sweet piety aglow,
　Such as e'en cloisters rarely know,
Hast meekly shed a heavenly light.

"Mother,"—they called thee, tender name!
　"Mother,"—on earth; and such wert thou;
　And though from them thou art parted now,
Their tearful cry is still the same.

---

[1] She presided over this monastery for thirty-three years, and her rule was so gentle that the sisters gave her no other name than that of "Our good mamma." She died on the 26th of December, 1871.

AD

Aloisivm Rotelli Can.

OB LAVDATIONEM

IN PARENTALIBVS

CARMELI PASCVCCI EP. PTOLEMAIDEN.

HABITAM.

SI iucunda tibi mea vox, excudere et acri
 Forte tuo igniculos, docte ROTELLE, novos

Si potis ingenio; meritae cape munera laudis
 Et cape Pastoris praescia vota tui.

CARMELVM immiti celebras dum funere ademptum,
 Vim morbi infandam dum pius illacrimas,

To Canon Aloysius Rotelli,

COMMENDATORY OF HIS EULOGY ON THE

MOST REV. CARMELO PASCUCCI,

ARCHBISHOP OF PTOLEMAIS.

IF voice of mine with pleasure thrill
Thy heart to me devoted still;
If song of mine may e'en inspire
Thy genius to enlarge its fire;
Take, sage Rotelli, take these lays
    To desert a tribute due:
    I have beat them out for praise,
    I have beat them out for you;
Oh! take thy Shepherd's tokens true.

Lo! while you pay Carmelo's bier
The meed of a commending tear,
And mournful rue death's cruel doom
That rudely bore him to the tomb;

Spectandumque refers doctrinae foenore multo,
    Insignem meritis et pietate virum,

Maiestate gravem et vultum, dum rite litanti
    Ornaret niveas infula sacra comas;

Atque itidem studia et mores animumque benignum,
    Os et suave senis, flexile et ingenium;

Sic graphice pingis divina rhetoris arte,
    Illo ut sit praesul nullus amabilior:

Ora immota tenens, arrectaque aure loquentem
    Te quisque admirans suspicit atque stupet.

Ipse sed in primis blanda dulcedine tangor,
    Exsultoque animis laetus, et usque memor,

Lo! while you paint with wealth of art,
Matchless merits, matchless mind,
Praise the virtues of the heart,
Looks wherein there sat enshrined
Grace, majesty with grace combined.

—Chief, when with hallowed fillet dight,
And mitred locks all snowy white,
And eyes commercing with the skies,
He sped the rightful sacrifice—:
While thus you trace with wit divine
Goodly gifts, majestic mien,
And the wonted smile benign
Sunshine of a soul serene,
Of one who left no peer, I ween;

See, wondering throngs in mute amaze,
With struggling breath and spell-bound gaze,
Are hearkening with delight intense
To thy enchanting eloquence.
But oh! how my glad heart is blest
With a sweet reflective joy;
Oh! what memories fill my breast,
Memories time cannot destroy
Of how I loved thee when a boy;

Te puerum fovisse sinu, vitaeque recentis
    Afflaret roscas cum levis aura genas,

Fulgidulosque micare oculos, vultumque decorum,
    Membraque conspicerem nescia stare loco,

Clamasse : eia ! adolesce puer, felicibus ausis
    I quo vivida te mens animusque rapit.

Delapsa e caelo tibi Pieris una Sororum
    Frondis Apollineae cingat honore caput :

Te verbo Suadela potens, te abstrusa Mathesis
    Cultorem iactent invida quaeque suum :

Now bringing back the gladsome time
Of blushing boyhood's happy prime,
When life's fresh springtide zephyrs blew
Into thy cheeks their roseate hue;
When first I saw those flashing eyes,
      Living stars of purest ray
      Kindling in their parent skies,
      With a face like morn in May
And elfish limbs ne'er tired of play.

Yes, memory fond recalls again
The very wish I breathed thee then:
"Spring up, bright boy! to manhood's prime:
On, onward speed to deeds sublime,
Aloft by native genius borne.
      May the heaven-descended Maid
      Thee with Phoebus' gifts adorn —
      Bays, whose bright Pierian braid
Was plucked the poet's brow to shade.

Let Eloquence, whose forceful art
Hath power to sway the human heart,
With arduous Mathematics claim
Alliance jealous with thy name.

Post, ubi vernantes maturior egeris annos,
  Pleno haustu Sophiae sacra fluenta bibas,

Qua duce, dura pati, moliri fortia discas
  Tangere et excelso vertice summa poli.

And when thy youth its bloom has shed,
    And the lights of manhood shine,
    Seek the sacred fountain-head
    Flowing fast by Wisdom's shrine,
Still thirsting quaff the draught divine;

Oh! learn from Wisdom lessons rare:
    Learn to struggle and to bear,
    Learn undying deeds to dare,
    Learn from lowly earth to rise,
And touch with towering crest the skies."

AD

Ieremiam Brvnelli

RHETOREM.

DVM Senae Adriacis, Cancri sub sidere, in undis
Mersor, caerulei mulcet et aura freti,

Me salvere iubes, et pignus mittis amoris,
Vota, adfert IOACHIM quae mihi sacra dies.

Quae sit par dono, dulci iucunda poetae,
Quae, Brunelli, animo gratia digna tuo?

Carmina carminibus, votis et vota rependam:
Te bonus incolumem sospitet usque Deus.

To Jeremiah Brunelli,

PROFESSOR OF RHETORIC.

O'ER Adriatic waters as I go
'Neath starry Crab, while soft sea breezes blow,

Fair greeting sendest thou; this festal day
JOACHIM brings thy loving tribute-lay.

What meed, dear poet, can thy gifts requite?
Since naught of mine can match thy love's behight.

Rhymes answer Rhymes, let vows thy vows repay
May bounteous God e'er guard and guide thy way.

Damnatorvm ad Inferos

LAMENTABILIS VOX.

" O si daretur hora ! "

AVDITVS stygiis gemitus resonare sub antris,
—O detur miseris hinc procul hora brevis.—

Quid facerent? Imo elicerent e corde dolorem,
Admissum et scelus abstergeret hora brevis.

The Doleful Cry of the Damned.

"Oh, for an hour's reprieve!"

WITHIN the Stygian caves is heard a piercing wail,
Oh, for one hour's reprieve, far from this pool of bale!

What would be done? From out the heart repentant teen
Would spring: that hour from stain of sin would leave it
  clean.

In Gallvm [1]

SIBI LICENTIVS INDVLGENTEM.

GALLE quid insanis? quid te torpere veterno,
    Diffluere illecebris deliciisque iuvat?

Puber, adhuc prima adspersus lanugine malas,
    Deperis incautum captus amore Cloen.

Grandior ecce Bycen ardes mollemque Corynnam,
    Inque dies vulnus saevior ignis alit.

Iamque senescentem, miseroque cupidine fractum
    Nunc premit indigno vafra Nigella iugo.

Ecquis erit modus? E coeno caput exere tandem,
    Tandem, rumpe moras, excute corde luem.

To Gallus.[1]

WHAT madness, Gallus! Why this torpid soul
That yields its life to wanton love's control?

A boy with downy cheek and downier wit,
Love's fever-flame within thee Chloe lit;

A man, and still to fan the amorous fire
Gay Byce and Corinna soft conspire;

A greybeard now, distempered passion's wreck,
Unshamed to be at shrewd Nigella's beck.

Is there no end? Come, from thy torpor start;
Come, shake the burning fever from thy heart.

Cunctaris, veteresque amens sectaris amores?
Iam spes heu misero nulla salutis adest.

Praedam inhians rabidus lateri stat demon, amara
Te mors, te vindex Numinis ira manet.

---

[1] Virum Perusinum intellige, quem ad sanitatem revocare Episcopus diu studuit.

Dost shrink thy veteran vices to forswear?
Doomed man! there's naught to stay thy sheer despair.

Grim Death and fierce Perdition summon thee,
The avengers dire of outraged Deity.

[1] A gentleman of Perugia whom the Bishop made frequent efforts to reclaim from dissolute habits.

Ars Photographica.

EXPRESSA solis spiculo
    Nitens imago, quam bene
    Frontis decus, vim luminum
    Refers, et oris gratiam.

O mira virtus ingeni
    Novumque monstrum! Imaginem
    Naturae Apelles aemulus
    Non pulchriorem pingeret.

On a Photograph.

SUN-WROUGHT image! All may see
Bright and beaming writ in thee
Gracious features, thought-crowned brow,
Eyes with living light aglow.

Modern wit is master here:
Not Appelles, Nature's peer,
Could with truer pencil trace
Thy unlabored, clear-cut grace.

Ad Prael. Orfei.

LUSUS POETICUS.

MULCERE immites cithara, deducere cantu,
Orpheu, fama refert te potuisse feras.

Pristina num virtus renovat portenta? nepotes
Gloria sollicitat numquid avita tuos?

Crediderim : Samut visus novus Orpheus oris
Elicere arguta dulce melos cythara.

Laevaque ab Adriaca advolitans regione columba
Nostro, heu, cum pullis in lare nidificat.

To Monsignor Orfei.[1]

EPIGRAM.

ORPHEUS, in days of old, they say
  Such strains from thy sweet lyre would well
  That beasts, in haste from brake and fell
Followed, enravished by thy lay.

Can power like this its portents show
  In sons of thine who sing to-day?
  Yea, sooth, for wields a kindred sway
A Samnian Orpheus whom I know.

And now from Adriatic shore,
  With baleful omen fluttering here
  A Dove—alas! its brood to rear,
Builds a trim nest above our door.

---

[1] Mons. Orfei, the author's predecessor in the Government of Benevento, had given up a part of the Apostolic Palace, called the Castle, to the President of the Tribunal, the barrister Palomba who had come from Loretto. It may further be noted for the benefit of the English reader, that the point of the epigram lies in the name of Palomba which is the Italian for a wild-dove.

De Se Ipso.[1]

JUSTITIAM colui: certamina longa, labores,
   Ludibria, insidias, aspera quaeque tuli.
At fidei vindex non flector: pro grege Christi
   Dulce pati, ipsoque in carcere dulce mori.

---

[1] Inscriptio effigiei suae apposita a Pontifice Maximo Leone XIII.

On Himself.[1]

JUSTICE I sought; and toil and lengthened strife
And taunts and wiles and every hardship, life
Have burdened : I Faith's champion do not bend ;
For Christ's flock sweet the pain, sweet — life in bonds to
   end.

----

[1] An Inscription written on a portrait of himself by Leo XIII.

ADMISSUS nuper est ad Pontificem Maximum Leonem XIII quidam nobili genere adolescens, decimum sextum aetatis annum vix supergressus: idemque macilento ore, et extenuatis viribus. Quod cum ipse licentioris vitae intemperantia factum non dissimularet, et dolenter ferre videretur, admonitus est, prospiceret saluti suae, opportuneque in asceterium aliquamdiu secederet, eluendis animae sordibus unice vacaturus. Id quo facilius assequeretur, suasit adolescenti Pontifex ut qua maxima posset attentione perlegeret aureum illum de quatuor *Hominis Novissimis* librum, scilicet auctore Dyonisio Carthusiano, qui copia et sanctitate doctrinae *Divini* nomen invenit. Eam Pontifex rem his, qui sequuntur versibus amplexus est.

Mense Majo anno MDCCCLXXXIV.

Not long since there was admitted into the presence of His Holiness, Pope Leo XIII, a young nobleman, scarcely out of his sixteenth year, yet wearing a haggard look and showing an extremely weakened frame of body. As he made no effort to conceal the fact that his pitiful appearance was the result of his dissolute manner of living, and seemed keenly to appreciate the misery to which he saw himself reduced; the Holy Father gave him a kind but strong admonition to have a serious regard for his welfare both spiritual and physical, and with this view, to retire for a while to some religious house where he might devote himself solely to cleansing his soul of its defilements. As a help to him in this holy task, he urged him to read with careful reflection the golden volume "On the Four Last Things," written by Denis the Carthusian, who has merited the title of the *Divine* by the richness and holiness of his doctrine. The Pontiff has given poetical expression to this little incident in the lines that follow.

Ad Florum.[1]

FLORE puer, vesana diu te febris adurit:
    Inficit immundo languida membra situ
Dira lues; cupidis stygio respersa veneno,
    Nec pudor est, labiis pocula plena bibis.
Pocula sunt Circes: apparent ora ferarum;
    Sus vel amica luto, vel truculentus aper.
Si sapis, o tandem miser expergiscere, tandem,
    Ulla tuae si te cura salutis habet.
Heu fuge Sirenum cantus, fuge litus avarum
    Et te Carthusi, Flore, reconde sinu
Haec tibi certa salus; Carthusi e fontibus hausta[1]
    Continuo sordes proluet unda tuas.

———— - —

[1] Ex consideratione scilicet rerum, quae sunt homini novissimae.

To Florus.[1]

FLORUS, a fever wastes thee with its fire:
 In deepest languor steeped, droops thy young frame:
Cups, brimming with Hell's poison of desire,
  Give to thy eager lips a draught of shame;
  Circean cups, that make thee look the same
As brutish swine, enamored of the mire,
  Or sullen boars, whose savage eyeballs flame—
With frenzied purpose wrought by blinding ire—
Ah, hapless boy! awake, awake at length!
  If thou canst still the cry of reason hear,
  And look thee to the welfare of thy soul!
Fly Siren voices, fly, with all thy strength!
  Within Carthusian walls seek fountains clear:
  [1]There cleansing thoughts and deeds shall make thee whole.

——— --

[1] Namely, the consideration of the Four Last Things.

Auspicatus Ecclesiae Triumphus.

AUGUROR: apparent flammantia lumina coelo,
Sidereoque rubens fulget ab axe dies.

Continuo effugiunt, subitoque exterrita visu
Tartareos repetunt horrida monstra lacus.

Gens inimica Deo portentum invita fateri,
Fletuque admissum visa piare scelus.

Tunc veteres cecidere irae, tunc pugna quievit:
Pectora mox dulci foedere iungit amor.

The Triumph of the Church Foreshadowed.

THUS do I prophesy: a flaming light
E'en now with radiance bathes the eastern sky,
And from the starry heavens flashing bright
The rosy dawn lights up the glistening eye.

Then straightway to the nether pools of fire
The hated monsters plunge affrighted down :
And in the fetid, ever-burning mire
Sink once again with many a horrid groan.

Constrained, at length, this wonder to confess
The race that waged erewhile relentless strife
Against its God, turns now that God to bless
And mourn the errors of its sinful life.

Then hatred long indulged and bitter grown
And angry combating against the right
Cease, and by virtue's magic power won
All hearts in blissful harmony unite.

Quin et prisca redit pietas, neglectaque virtus,
    Candida pax, castusque et sine fraude pudor.

Illustrat vetus illa Italas sapientia mentes:
    Longius errorum pulsa caterva cohors.

O laeta Ausoniae tellus! o clara triumpho,
    Et cultu et patria relligione potens!

Nay men who scorned to love with fervor burn
    And virtue's path bestrewn with roses find,
Peace once again and modesty return
    And the sweet face, that speaks the guileless mind.

That wisdom which so brilliant shone of eld
    Upon us now an equal lustre sheds,
And error, by new charity repelled,
    No longer through the land infection spreads.

O fair Ausonian land! O happy home!
    O crowned with glory and with victory!
O powerful in the glorious faith of Rome,
    The birthright dear, that Peter left to thee!

Frustrata Impiorum Spe

OCCIDIT, inclamant, solio dejectus, in ipso
Carcere, in aerumnis occidit ecce Leo.

Spes insana: Leo alter adest, qui sacra volentes
Jura dat in populos, imperiumque tenet.

The Hope of the Wicked is Vain.

THE LINE OF THE ROMAN PONTIFFS IS UNBROKEN.

"CAST down from throne to prison cell
    Leo has fallen," their joyful refrain,
        "Has fallen midst sadness and sorrow."
Ah vain is the hope of the infidel!
    Over glad Rome a new Leo shall reign,
        And rule as Christ's Vicar to-morrow.

www.ingramcontent.com/pod-product-compliance
Lightning Source LLC
Chambersburg PA
CBHW021118020726
47500CB00003B/820